*Princess Giselle didn't know
his real name or anything about him.
She only knew he had made her
feel utterly alive and desirable*

Would she feel the same once the masks were off? The mystery might be what made him so enticing. Somehow, she doubted it. Something in him had called her, soul to soul, like a voice in her mind, promising the earth if only she was open to the possibilities….

She wanted to meet him, to stare into his eyes and discover if the spell was really there, or only existed in her mind.

Midnight was only seconds away and some people were already reaching to undo their masks. Her gaze became frantic. Where was he?

Laughter bubbled around her as faces were revealed, some expected, some obviously causing surprise. Nowhere could she see her mystery man.

He had vanished as if into her imagination.

Dear Reader,

Egad! This month we're up to our eyeballs in royal romances!

In *Fill-In Fiancée* (#1694) by DeAnna Talcott, a British lord pretends marriage to satisfy his parents. But will the hasty union last? Only time will tell, but matchmaker Emily Winters has her fingers crossed and so do we! This is the third title of Silhouette Romance's exclusive six-book series, MARRYING THE BOSS'S DAUGHTER.

In *The Princess & the Masked Man* (#1695), the second book of Valerie Parv's THE CARRAMER TRUST miniseries, a clever princess snares the affections of a mysterious single father. Look out for the final episode in this enchanting royal saga next month.

Be sure to make room on your reading list for at least one more royal. *To Wed a Sheik* (#1696) is the last title in Teresa Southwick's exciting DESERT BRIDES series. A jaded desert prince is no match for a beautiful American nurse in this tender and exotic romance.

But if all these royal romances have put you in the mood for a good old-fashioned American love story, look no further than *West Texas Bride* (#1697) by bestselling author Madeline Baker. It's the story of a city girl who turns a little bit country to win the heart of her brooding cowboy hero.

Enjoy!

Mavis C. Allen
Associate Senior Editor

Please address questions and book requests to:
Silhouette Reader Service
U.S.: 3010 Walden Ave., P.O. Box 1325, Buffalo, NY 14269
Canadian: P.O. Box 609, Fort Erie, Ont. L2A 5X3

The Princess & the Masked Man

VALERIE PARV

THE CARRAMER TRUST

SILHOUETTE *Romance*®

Published by Silhouette Books

America's Publisher of Contemporary Romance

For the wonderful hosts at eHarlequin
who keep us in touch and on our toes.

SILHOUETTE BOOKS

ISBN 0-373-19695-4

THE PRINCESS & THE MASKED MAN

Copyright © 2003 by Valerie Parv

This edition published by arrangement with Harlequin Books S.A.

® and TM are trademarks of Harlequin Books S.A., used under license. Trademarks indicated with ® are registered in the United States Patent and Trademark Office, the Canadian Trade Marks Office and in other countries.

Visit Silhouette at www.eHarlequin.com

Printed in U.S.A.

VALERIE PARV

With 20 million copies of her books sold, including three Waldenbooks' bestsellers, it's no wonder Valerie Parv is known as Australia's queen of romance, and is the recognized media spokesperson for all things romantic. Valerie is married to her own romantic hero, Paul, a formal crocodile hunter in Australia's tropical north.

These days he's a cartoonist and the two live in the country's capital city of Canberra, where both are volunteer zoo guides, sharing their love of animals with visitors from all over the world. Valerie continues to write her page-turning novels because they affirm her belief in love and happy endings. As she says, "Love gives you wings, romance helps you fly." Keep up with Valerie's latest releases at www.silromanceauthors.com.

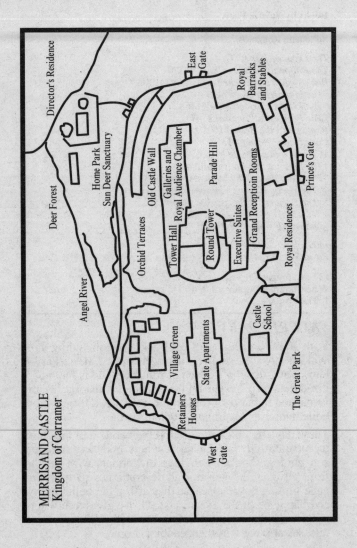

MERRISAND CASTLE
Kingdom of Carramer

Director's Residence

Deer Forest

Angel River

Home Park
Sun Deer Sanctuary

Orchid Terraces

Old Castle Wall

Tower Hall

Galleries and
Royal Audience Chamber

Round Tower

Parade Hill

East Gate

Royal Barracks and Stables

Executive Suites

Grand Receptioin Rooms

Royal Residences

Prince's Gate

Retainers' Houses

Village Green

State Apartments

Castle School

The Great Park

West Gate

Prologue

Bryce Laws fumbled with his black tie and bit his tongue to keep from swearing out loud. "You could lend a hand instead of watching me suffer," he grumbled.

His daughter crossed the room with a grace that belied her ten years. Reaching up, she tied the tie with deft efficiency. "There, how's that?"

He regarded the neat result in the mirror. He still looked like a penguin, but at least he was a properly attired one. "The ability to tie one of these things must be bred into women. Your mother…"

Hearing his voice tail off, Amanda smiled wanly. "It's okay, Dad, you can talk about her. I won't come apart on you. I'm over that now."

The harshness of her words didn't conceal the hurt he heard beneath them. "You still miss her, don't you, chicken?" He certainly did, even two years on.

"Sure. She wouldn't have let you bring me to this place."

He dropped a hand to her shoulder. How delicate she was, this half child, half woman he had sired. Yvette's long illness had forced Amanda to grow up far too quickly. He had hoped taking a job at Merrisand Castle and giving her the opportunity to act her age around other children would give her back some of her interrupted childhood. After a month at Merrisand, the plan wasn't working too well. "You're still determined to hate the castle?"

She affected a shrug. "The deer park is cool. It reminds me of our old place. Sometimes I pretend we're back there and everything's the way it was. But the castle school stinks."

She wasn't the only one who regretted the changes in their life, he thought. He had also loved Eden Valley, their property on the beautiful, fertile island of Nuee. When his parents returned to America to be with his grandfather after a yachting accident had left him confined to a wheelchair, Bryce had taken over management of the ranch. Amanda had been three then, Yvette had been healthy and as excited as he was at the prospect of having Eden Valley to themselves. It hadn't exactly turned out the way they'd dreamed.

He shrugged into the jacket of his dinner suit. There were some things he wouldn't want back the way they had been, such as his grandfather's constant interference from afar. Amanda didn't know how frustrated Bryce had been, having the old man second-guess him about every major decision.

Reminding Karl Laws that Bryce and his parents were also shareholders in the family company that owned Eden Valley hadn't helped. As long as Karl held the controlling interest—*controlling* being the operative word—he was the real boss. From his wheelchair, he ruled the American side of the Laws business empire through his son, and the Carramer side through his grandson.

No, there were some things Bryce didn't miss.

He pulled himself back to the present. "Define stinks."

Amanda made a face. "The castle school is *soooo* stuffy. It's all history, history, history. You'd think Carramer had more past than future."

Sometimes he felt the same about himself. "You study modern subjects, I know you do."

She gave a snort of derision. "Like you'd know."

He felt a smile start. "I went to school in Carramer, too, admittedly in the Dark Ages."

She grinned in spite of herself. The transformation was astonishing. From a surly child, she became a real beauty. With the striking blond coloring and glorious hair she had inherited from her mother, Bryce didn't doubt she'd be a heartbreaker one day. "Thirty isn't all that ancient, Dad. If we'd moved somewhere more exciting than Merrisand, you might have married again," she said.

"I'm not interested in marrying again." Seeing her face darken, he regretted his sharp tone. Was she trying to tell him she wouldn't mind if he did? He touched the back of his hand to her cheek as if he could erase the downcast expression. "I have all the family I need right here."

He couldn't imagine risking a repeat of the heartache he'd endured during Yvette's illness. Amanda had been five when Yvette was stricken with a mysterious blood disease no doctor could diagnose or cure. His heart still bled to think of his wife's battle to live as the disease took her away in slow, painful increments.

Twice she had rallied, giving them hope that one of the desperate treatments they'd tried might be working. In the end nothing had, and she had slipped away two years before. The wound in Bryce's heart felt less raw now, but in a way that was more alarming. Would he eventually be left feeling nothing at all?

Bryce had expected his grandfather to understand his difficulties, since Karl had lost his own wife to a stroke a decade before. Instead, the specter of Yvette's illness had seemed to frighten Karl. He had become even more despotic, making no allowances for the vast amounts of time and money Bryce had needed to devote to seeking a cure.

Not surprisingly, the running of Eden Valley had suffered, displeasing Karl so much that he had used his majority vote to have the land put up for auction. Maybe he had intended the threat to bring his grandson to heel. But Bryce was more like his grandfather than either of them wanted to admit, and had surprised the old man by agreeing that selling was the best option. His parents had taken more convincing that Bryce really did want to strike out on his own before they also voted in favor of selling. The sale had gone through five months ago.

The auction was the reason he and Amanda were living at Merrisand, he mused. Prince Maxim de Marigny, the administrator of the castle and its estates, had attended the auction to inspect Eden Valley's renowned stock of Mayat deer, a cross between Chital and Carramer's native sun deer. Bryce had spent a lot of time with the prince, preferring to talk about deer breeding than focus on what was happening to Eden Valley. Evidently he had impressed the prince, because soon after the auction Maxim invited Bryce to take over management of the Royal Deer Park at Merrisand.

Bryce planned to build the park up until the herds were the equal of those he'd bred at Eden Valley. Then he intended to use his share of the auction proceeds plus whatever he could save working for the royal family to buy another ranch and start again. Prince Maxim had given him complete authority over the royal park, but it wasn't the same as having a place he and Amanda could call their own.

He could have taken her to live in America. His mother had been born on Nuee, but his father was American. Bryce himself had dual citizenship, having been born in America after he arrived early when his parents were visiting his grandparents. But Carramer was where he belonged. Yvette's parents lived on Nuee but were still coming to terms with her death. Another reason he had for being glad he had brought Amanda to Merrisand.

"At least you'll finally get to meet Princess Giselle," she said now.

He sat on the edge of the bed and pulled on the black shoes he'd polished until they gleamed. Normally the princess assisted her brother, Maxim, with the running of the castle. When Bryce arrived, he'd been told she was away in Taures city nursing an injured foot. She hadn't summoned him to her presence on her return, so either she was happy with her brother's appointment of Bryce, or she had more pressing priorities. Either way, she would be too busy with her many guests to pay him much heed tonight.

"There will be a lot of people at the ball. I probably won't see much of the princess." The only reason he was putting himself through the ordeal was because all senior castle employees were expected to attend. He was also curious, he had to admit. Was the princess as beautiful as he'd been told?

Amanda curled up at the head of the bed like a kitten. "You'll be the best-looking man there, and the princess will be swept away."

He slanted a look at the black mask lying between them. "I'm not sure how she's supposed to tell."

"Women know these things," she said airily. "Don't you think a masked ball is romantic?"

"Easy for you to say, chicken. You're not the one who has to turn up looking like Zorro."

"How about the Phantom of the Opera?"

"Or the Lone Ranger?"

"A superhero," she countered.

With a sigh of resignation, he slipped the mask over his face and stood up to check the effect in the mirror. As a boy he had wondered how superheroes got away without being recognized. Now he was amazed at the difference the black mask made to his appearance. With only his eyes and mouth visible, he looked mysterious and totally unlike himself. Attending the princess's ball was still an ordeal he could do without, but seeing himself in the mask made him feel marginally better about it.

The doorbell pealed. "That will be Mrs. Gray." Their housekeeper, normally only there during the daytime, had agreed to sit with Amanda tonight.

The child bounced off the bed. "I'm old enough not to need a sitter, you know."

He ruffled her hair. "Humor me. I need the reassurance."

At his bedroom door, she turned back. "You look great, Dad. You're going to knock Princess Giselle's socks off."

Amanda assumed he wanted to. He made a shooing gesture. "Go and let Mrs. Gray in so I can get this evening over with."

Chapter One

This was a crazy idea, Giselle thought as she surveyed the assembled guests from the swaying height of the sedan chair borne on the shoulders of four members of the Royal Protection Detail. She should never have let her equerry talk her into making her entrance this way.

Not that she had needed much persuading. The alternative, hobbling in leaning on a cane, hadn't held much appeal.

Torn ligaments and a chipped bone had been the doctor's verdict after a horse she'd been riding at an official function threw her heavily. After the plaster was removed, she'd been ordered to rest her foot for another month. Merrisand Castle, built on a hill, was too difficult for her to get around in that condition, so she had spent the time at her parents' home in Taures city. She was thankful she had only needed a plaster cast for the first two weeks, or she would have been delivered to the ball in a wheelchair.

She didn't know what was hardest to endure: the lack of mobility or being fussed over by her mother. Princess Marie meant well, Giselle knew, but as consort to the governor of Taures, and aunt to the country's reigning monarch, she was far more earnest about her royal role than Giselle would ever be.

Marie had a never-ending list of rules for how a princess should behave. Falling off a horse was definitely not one of them. What was Giselle supposed to do, stick to riding sidesaddle? Probably, she thought gloomily.

It was bad enough being reminded constantly of archaic rules such as "a lady only ever has one leg." This was usually said when Giselle was wearing jeans and seated with her legs comfortably apart instead of crossed in one neat line as her mother's rule demanded. Was she also supposed to give up all the healthy activities she enjoyed in favor of more ladylike pursuits like needlework? Fat chance.

Now was not the time to worry about such things, she told herself, feeling her spirits lift. She was home again in her beloved Merrisand Castle in time to host her favorite charity ball of the year. If she had to make her entrance in a sedan chair, so be it. This was supposed to be a fantasy affair anyway.

She looked around. The women shimmered in their designer gowns, the men looking incredibly handsome in black tie. Everyone seemed more glamorous and mysterious behind their masks. She recognized a few people even with their masks, but many faces had her puzzled. Was that really her brother, Maxim, wearing a stylish black cape over his evening dress, his mask revealing only his mouth and strong jaw?

She suspected that he was frowning at her as usual.

Probably disapproving of her unorthodox mode of transport. If she couldn't draw all eyes with her dancing prowess, she had to settle for making an entrance. She caught a cheerful grin from the man beside him. Eduard de Marigny, the present marquis of Merrisand. Masked or not, she would know him anywhere. It was a pity he lived in Valmont Province when he wasn't serving with the Carramer navy because he was one of Giselle's staunchest supporters.

Beside him was his wife, Carissa. Giselle could see her cornflower eyes sparkling behind a tiny feathered mask. Carissa had met Eduard and love had blossomed between them after she mistakenly purchased one of the royal homes from a con man. Giselle was godmother to their adorable triplets, Jamet, Michelle and Henry, and counted Carissa as a dear friend. She exchanged smiles with the other woman.

Because this was a masked ball, there was no receiving line and Giselle was truly grateful. She had an excellent memory and could usually call to mind a few personal details about each of the guests as they were presented to her, but it was a tedious task. Much more challenging to try to guess who everyone was before the masks were due to come off at midnight.

After setting her down carefully at the head of the ballroom, the four members of the R.P.D. who had carried her stepped away from the chair and fanned out to keep an unobtrusive watch for the rest of the night. At her signal, trays of champagne and canapés were carried around, and the orchestra struck up the first dance of the evening. As she tapped her injured foot in instinctive response to the music, a twinge of pain reminded her that she wouldn't be joining the other couples on the floor. She stilled her foot, feeling frustration settle over her like a cloud.

Her royal relatives were dancing or talking, and the other guests had left a deferential circle of space around her. She restrained the urge to tell them to come closer, she didn't bite. Feeling isolated was a fact of royal life.

Normally she would have circulated among the crowd, putting others at ease until she felt that way herself. It was one of her mother's rules that she actually found sensible. Limited by her injury, she could only look pleasant and hope someone would have the sense to approach her.

"Can I get you something, Your Highness?"

Expecting one of the servants, she looked up. And up, and up. Then felt her breath catch. The man beside her was a couple of inches over six feet tall, with a muscular build and long, athletic legs that looked as if they would eat up a dance floor. Like the other male guests, he wore evening dress and on him it looked dashingly individual.

And his eyes.

Behind his mask they were a clear, dark blue like the waters of a bottomless lake, and just as unfathomable. They met hers with a directness she seldom experienced other than from members of her family. He didn't act like one of the castle staff, she thought, struggling to put a name to what she could see of his face. He must be a friend of Maxim or Eduard. No employee would meet her gaze so unflinchingly, as if daring her to accept him as anything other than an equal.

His hair was as black as midnight, the slightly untamed strands skimming the collar of his pristine dress shirt. The contrast was startling. Only an hour ago, she had joked with her lady-in-waiting about meeting her Prince Charming at the ball, never expecting it to be a possibility.

It wasn't a possibility now, although it was difficult to remember, when her heart thudded against her chest and her breath felt strangled. He was only another guest, although he looked as if he had stepped straight out of her dreams.

''I don't—that is, I'd better not in case I have to resort to pain medication during the evening.'' She was furious with herself for stumbling over the words.

She imagined eyebrows as black as his hair winging upward beneath the mask. ''Are you in pain now?''

His concerned tone provoked a frisson of response. ''Nothing to worry about.'' The faint twinge had been forgotten at her first sight of him.

He gestured at the sedan chair. ''Unusual mode of transportation.''

She could have kissed him for offering the conversational lifeline, then almost sighed at the thought. Kissing him would be an extraordinary experience. One she wasn't in the least likely to have. It didn't stop her from imagining his generous mouth claiming hers, their breath mingling.

It had been a long time since she'd been kissed by anyone. Really kissed. There was Robert, of course. But he never made her feel this confused or needy. Maybe that's why she felt driven to end the relationship. She wanted a man who made her feel more than he did.

The way she felt now.

She gathered her scattered wits. Although her medication had been tapered almost to nothing, it must be to blame for her confusion. How else to explain the fast hammering of her heart, and her sense that the ballroom was overheated suddenly?

She tried for a normal tone. "The sedan chair is a museum piece that belonged to my grandmother, Princess Antoinette. I had to choose between using the chair or a walking stick."

"I saw the chair on display in the Tower Hall a couple of days ago and wondered how riding in it would feel," he observed.

"Bumpy." His voice reminded her of hot chocolate, smooth, rich, delicious.

She gave a barely perceptible shake of her head to clear it. It wasn't done to seek introductions at a masked ball and take the mystery out of the occasion, but she found herself wanting to. She settled for saying, "We haven't met before. Are you staying at the castle?"

He inclined his head. "For the moment."

An answer that told her precisely nothing about him. "I would like some sparkling water," she said, feeling her mouth dry.

She regretted the request when he turned away from her at once. Stay, she wanted to command, feeling a sense of desertion sweep over her. Then she retracted the thought, as watching him brought its own gratification.

He moved with a controlled strength that was like poetry, muscles fluid under the black suit. A man of action, she decided, one used to having his body obey him without thought. When he brought her glass of water, his fingers looked strong around the fragile flute. He gave it to her and a tingle traveled through her as his hand brushed hers.

Trying not to show how unnerved she was, she said, "Thank you."

His dark gaze swept the crowd around them. "This can't be much fun for you, Your Highness."

Something in his gaze inspired her confidence. "It beats spending two months with my mother."

A sparkle of understanding lit the blue depths. "Prince Maxim told me you were staying at Taures Palace. I gather it wasn't a picnic."

He must be one of her brother's guests, she concluded. All the same she shouldn't be discussing her family with someone she didn't know, although she was tempted to do just that. "What's the old saying? 'You can't go home again.'"

Did she imagine the sudden tightening around his mouth? All he said was, "Quite." He shifted as if to move away.

"Stay and talk to me," she said, shocking herself slightly. Feeling needy was one thing, but indulging it with a stranger was quite another. Her mother was bound to have a rule against such behavior.

He inclined his head in silent acknowledgment. "I don't wish to monopolize your time. Protocol…"

"To blazes with protocol," she said, then moderated her tone, "As you can see, there's not much competition for my attention."

He took a sip of champagne. "Perhaps they're intimidated by you."

"Because of the sedan chair?" It did look somewhat like a throne, she conceded.

"Sitting in that thing, you look terrifyingly regal."

"You don't seem intimidated."

His deep blue eyes shone. "Fishing, Princess? All identities remain a mystery until midnight."

"Wondering," she compromised. "No law against that, is there?"

"Not unless your family chooses to make one."

"You aren't going to give me any clues, are you?" He had already given one when he'd mentioned Maxim so familiarly. "Are you a friend of Max's?"

All he admitted was, "I know the prince."

All the guests were connected by their association with the castle, either as members of the Merrisand Trust like her and Max, friends who supported the trust's charitable work, or senior members of the royal household. "The same may be said of anyone here."

"True enough."

She found she liked the sensation of sparring with him. "You have me at an unfair advantage. You know who I am, but I don't even know what to call you."

He seemed to think for a moment. "You could try Clark."

"Although it isn't your real name." She didn't know how she knew, only that she did.

"My daughter put the idea in my head when I was getting ready this evening."

A stab of disappointment lanced through her. So he was married with a child. She should have known. "You should be grateful she didn't suggest something more bizarre."

She saw the corners of his mouth lift. "Considering the alternatives the mask suggested to her, Clark was the mildest option."

A flash of inspiration made her ask, "As in the superhero?"

He looked discomfited. ''It was the association she made, however inaccurately.''

So he didn't think of himself as a superhero. He certainly looked the part. It wasn't hard to imagine him leaping tall buildings or rescuing maidens in distress. She really was getting fanciful tonight. He was married, remember? All the best ones were. He looked as averse to being at the ball as Giselle herself, probably because his wife wasn't at his side. ''I should circulate,'' she said, aware of sounding reluctant.

He glanced at her bandaged foot peeping from beneath the pearl-studded hem of her ball gown. Velvet-covered dance slippers had been the best she could do to accommodate the bandage. ''Unless you plan to tour the room from that chair, you might have some difficulty.'' He crooked an arm. ''I'm happy to offer my assistance.''

Provided she used a cane or other support for the time being, she could put weight on her injured foot now. And anything was better than being confined to this chair. Leaning on his strong arm was not her motivation for accepting, she assured herself. ''It would be good to move around for a while, but I don't want to impose,'' she said.

''Not at all, Your Highness. As you can see, there's hardly any competition for my attention.''

Hearing her own words turned back at her, she smiled. ''I mustn't take you away from your wife.''

What she could see of his face darkened fleetingly, then he returned her smile. ''With respect, you're fishing again. I can't help you do your duty as our hostess unless you agree to preserve the mystery.''

* * *

Bryce had no idea what had made him approach the princess, or why he hadn't come right out and admitted who he was. Some people might see the loss of Eden Valley as a comedown, but he regarded it as a liberation.

The next time he owned land, it would be in his own right, free of family interference. So, being an employee of the castle was a means to an end for him. But he found it hard to imagine the princess being so interested in him once she knew all about him. In spite of his vow to remain uninvolved, he was enjoying arousing her curiosity.

Arousing *her* might be even more of a challenge, not that he had any such intention. Although seeing her borne into the ball on the sedan chair carried by her protectors had certainly aroused him. Few women, even royalty, would have carried off such an entrance with her assurance.

During her stately progress into the ballroom, she had kept her back straight and her head high, exposing an expanse of swanlike neck. The full skirt of her strapless aquamarine gown had spilled over the runners of the chair, making it look as if she were floating on a cloud. He'd decided that he had to meet her.

She was right. He wasn't intimidated by her position. Coming from a family with interests in two countries, he was used to dealing with officials at the highest levels. Beyond business, he didn't usually seek them out, preferring the company of more everyday people like himself.

There was nothing everyday about Princess Giselle de Marigny.

For one thing her golden coloring set her apart. As fair as her brother was dark, she had eyes as bright as stars, of a jewel color he didn't have a name for. Her hair was wound into a chignon dressed with a diamond tiara. It wasn't a huge leap to imagine the strands tumbling around her shoulders in a riot of curls. Would they feel as silky as they looked, spilling through his fingers?

Her skin was like milk, shading to creamy pink under the rim of her jeweled mask, and she had the most tantalizing mouth. Soft, quick to smile. In a less public forum, he would have been sorely tempted to taste her. Maybe more than taste. Just as well he was constrained by the crowd.

When she took his hand and got carefully to her feet, she felt as light as his daughter, thistledown in a designer gown, a child masquerading as a princess. Except that there was nothing remotely childish in the smile she gave him as she curled her hand more securely around his arm. He felt his insides cramp in response.

"People will talk, you know," she murmured.

He crossed his free arm over his chest and covered her hand with his, telling himself it was the gentlemanly thing to do. It had nothing to do with welcoming any excuse to touch her. "Do you care, Your Highness?"

She gave a dismissive laugh. "If I let myself worry every time someone gossiped about me, I'd be a nervous wreck."

The only tremors he could feel in her were at his touch, possibly a product of his wishful thinking. "Then there's nothing to worry about, is there? Where would you like to begin?"

"My brother's group, if you'd kindly help me over to them."

Would Maxim recognize him and expose his identity to her? There was nothing for it but to comply. The prince was chatting amiably to a group, all masked as Bryce was. He hadn't been at the castle long enough to recognize many people, even without masks, so he didn't bother trying. Instead, he concentrated on Giselle's melodious conversation as she did her royal duty as hostess. Her presence had added an unexpected fillip to an occasion he hadn't expected to enjoy in the least.

The other guests were concerned about her, of course. Surprised to see her on her feet, Bryce gathered from their comments. "Clark kindly volunteered to help me get around," she said in a mischievous tone.

Bryce couldn't see Prince Maxim's frown of puzzlement as he tried to place the newcomer, but it was in his voice as he said, "Clark?"

"My secret identity for tonight, Your Highness," Bryce explained, feeling himself color under his own mask. Entertaining the princess was one thing. He hadn't planned on taking the joke any further.

"He came to my rescue when everyone else neglected me," she went on.

"The day you suffer neglect, my dear Giselle, the world comes to an end," Maxim observed. To Bryce, he said, "Normally I can't get near her for the men swarming around her."

"Perhaps when I'm able to dance," she grumbled. "Today I can barely manage a few steps without assistance."

Maxim's gaze went to her arm linked with Bryce's. "You don't seem to be suffering greatly at this moment."

He was right, she wasn't. Her foot throbbed, but the mystery of her benefactor's identity provided a welcome distraction. Maxim had given no sign that he recognized her escort, so her brother wasn't going to be much help. She would have to figure this out on her own.

Although she was consumed with curiosity about the imposing stranger, part of her wanted the mystery to continue. Behind the mask he could be any man she imagined, her Prince Charming if she so chose.

She told herself she was being capricious, but decided it couldn't hurt for one night. Soon she would be recovered enough to return to her royal duties. Added to the affairs of the trust, and her teaching commitments at the castle school, she would have little time for fantasy.

And that reminded her.

"I must arrange a meeting with you and Eduard, while he's still in Taures Province."

"Could we discuss that another time?" Maxim asked mildly enough, although Bryce heard the steely undercurrent in his tone.

Giselle's head came up. "You've avoided discussing it elsewhere, so you leave me little choice. Eduard returns to Valmont in two more days."

Bryce let his glance follow Maxim's to where a tall, dark-haired man was holding court. Eduard, Marquis of Merrisand, his prodigious memory supplied. He was so well known that no mask could conceal his identity.

Maxim made an impatient sound. "If it helps, I've already spoken to Eduard about your desire to be appointed Keeper of the Castle."

"And?"

Bryce heard the expectancy in her tone and wondered at it. Maxim presently held the dual titles of administrator of the Merrisand Trust and Keeper of the Castle. Giselle evidently hoped to take over the latter position herself. The Keeper was responsible for overseeing most of the day-to-day running of the castle, a big job for such slender shoulders, Bryce thought.

''We agree that you're well qualified, but Eduard is as constrained by the terms of the Merrisand Charter as I am,'' Maxim stated.

She turned to Bryce. ''What do you think of a charter created two hundred years ago that excludes women from the position of Keeper unless they are married?''

Bryce tried for diplomacy. ''I'd have to know more about the circumstances.''

She wasn't letting him off the hook so easily. ''What would you like to know?''

''For example, does the restriction apply only to women?''

''Unfortunately it does,'' Maxim interceded, sounding uneasy about the admission.

Bryce knew how his daughter would feel about that. Evidently the princess felt the same way. He didn't entirely blame her. He couldn't see the point of squandering half the world's talents through an accident of gender. Something he had been unable to make Amanda's maternal grandmother understand, or they might have parted on better terms. ''Can't the rules be updated?'' he asked.

''According to the charter, any changes must be put to the people of Taures province in a referendum. If they vote in favor, the change takes effect five years and one day from the date of the referendum.''

Too long for Giselle to wait, he gathered when he felt her tense on his arm. ''Isn't that a touch excessive?'' he asked.

''The charter's history is complicated,'' the princess said. ''Perhaps you know that the Merrisand title was conferred on our ancestor as an insult, after he fell out with the reigning monarch of the period.''

Bryce searched his memory. ''*Merrisand* being a term for a fool's paradise in Carramer folklore.'' In an effort to stir Amanda's interest in the move, he had suggested she research the castle's history on the Internet. She had gleefully reported the fool's paradise connection to him, sounding as if she thought the description still fitted.

''As I understand it, the first marquis turned the tables on his brother by establishing a charitable trust to help children in need, then built this castle to fund the trust's good works. What started out as an insult became one of the most respected names in the kingdom,'' he went on.

Giselle seemed pleased with his knowledge. ''Our ancestor had the five-year moratorium written into the charter to make sure the monarch couldn't meddle easily in the trust's affairs.''

''Those two really got along, didn't they?''

She sneaked a glance at her brother, whose attention had been claimed by another guest. ''Do you have brothers or sisters?''

''Not a one.'' After he was born his parents had tried for more children without success. Part of the reason for the intense interest his grandfather took in Bryce, he suspected. As his parents' sole heir, he carried all of his grandfather's expectations on his shoulders.

"Then you don't know how fierce sibling rivalry can get."

Although she couldn't see it, he lifted an eyebrow. "Even among royalty?"

"We're still human. Oh."

He felt her sag in his grasp and reached for a chair with his free hand, spinning it around so he could ease her into it. "Perhaps you should sit the rest of the ball out, Princess."

His hands on her arms felt so warm and confident that she wished she could spend the entire evening in his company. Not possible, of course. Her duty didn't permit it. Emboldened because she was now part of a group, other guests had begun to drift toward her.

When her mystery man stepped back to allow them to approach, it was all she could do not to grasp his hand and hold him at her side. She wanted to know who he was and why she found him so compelling.

At midnight, when the masks came off, she would have her answers, she promised herself as she pinned a smile of greeting to her face.

Ignoring the discomfort in her foot, she welcomed her guests and made polite conversation. Chatted, smiled until her jaw ached. Ate some of the lavish supper the castle chefs had created. Listened to the music and attempted not to feel too left out of the dancing.

And hoped she wasn't watching the clock too obviously.

Chapter Two

For the rest of the night, Bryce found it a strain being sociable. He knew why and he didn't like it. None of the other guests at the ball had captured his interest as totally as Princess Giselle.

It took enormous self-discipline to keep his glance from repeatedly straying to where she held court. The silvery peal of her laughter drew his attention like a magnet, making him pulse with desires he didn't want to feel. Not for any woman, but especially not for someone so inappropriate.

During the move to Merrisand, Amanda had shown him an article in a magazine linking the princess with one of Carramer's more famous exports, movie actor Robert Gaudet. He was in Hollywood at present, developing a new film project that his production company planned to make in Carramer. The article suggested that the princess's injury was the only thing preventing her from being with him. The actor was supposedly so much in love with her that their marriage was a foregone conclusion.

The article also mentioned the princess's many teaching and charitable activities for the Merrisand Trust and Bryce wondered how they would fit in with a Hollywood lifestyle.

He didn't normally pay attention to such things but had been prepared to encourage anything that made Amanda happier about the move to Merrisand. He had read the article to please her, deciding that his daughter could have a worse idol than the hardworking princess.

He tried to tell himself he was glad Giselle was involved with someone. Even if she hadn't been a princess, he had nothing to offer her, either emotionally or materially. His wife's illness had drained him of both the capacity and the will to put himself through such torment again. And until he put his financial affairs in order, he had little to offer any woman.

The logic didn't quench his desire to look at Giselle, and keep looking.

He thought he'd resisted the temptation fairly successfully until he became aware that his dance partner had stopped moving. He forced his attention back to her. ''Is something the matter?''

''Perhaps we should dance over to the other side of the room before you get a crick in your neck from turning that way.''

He had asked the woman to dance in order to banish Giselle from his mind. Giving her name as Elaine, she obviously expected Bryce to reciprocate. When he hadn't, she had volunteered that she was the princess's equerry and had been away in Taures with her boss until recently.

When Bryce reminded Elaine that their identities were supposed to remain secret until midnight, she had sounded frustrated but had danced with him readily enough. "You're new to Merrisand, aren't you?" she commented as he swung her into a waltz.

"Very." He knew she expected more from him, but didn't feel inclined to elaborate. He hadn't danced since Yvette became too ill, and was regretting the impulse to start again now. Not because Elaine wasn't a good dancer. She was light on her feet and followed his lead easily. And behind her striking gold mask, her features hinted at attractiveness. No, he was the problem, feeling uncomfortable holding her in his arms.

Strange. He hadn't felt that way when he assisted the princess earlier. She had fitted against his side as if she belonged there. Also missing was the tug of guilt he'd so often felt after catching himself enjoying some small pleasure. Yvette had been such a generous soul that she wouldn't want him to feel guilty on her account, yet he hadn't been able to dismiss the feeling.

Until this evening.

"My mind was wandering," he told Elaine. True enough.

"Flattery will get you everywhere," she murmured, matching her steps to his as he picked up the rhythm again.

"It's nothing personal. I'm out of practice at this." Also true.

"She is lovely, isn't she?" Elaine said.

He didn't insult her by pretending not to know who

she meant. "Yes. Also very popular." The crowd around Giselle had only lessened for the interval while supper was served.

"You wouldn't be the first man at the castle to fall in love with her."

Bryce felt his muscles tighten and made an effort to relax them. "You sound just like my daughter."

He could almost hear Elaine's thoughts as she added this up. Out of practice at dancing, and with a daughter. Therefore probably widowed or divorced. "How old is your daughter?"

As he heard the interest in her voice sharpen, he regretted even more asking her to dance. Then he reminded himself that he was the one using her to take his mind off the princess. "Ten, and an authority on celebrities, courtesy of her favorite magazine, *Fame and Fortune*."

"I read that magazine, too. They did an article recently about the princess and Robert Gaudet."

He nodded. "According to the writer, they're practically engaged."

Now who was fishing? he thought. As Giselle's right-hand woman, Elaine could be expected to know whether there was any truth in the article. He told himself he was merely curious.

Elaine's smile became artful. "You'd have to ask Her Highness about that."

He had to admire her discretion, although he couldn't help wondering who else her reticence was serving. As long as Giselle was committed to the actor, Bryce was wasting his time fantasizing about her. Especially when there was a lovely, available woman much closer to hand. Or so he could imagine Elaine wanting him to think.

Maybe she was right. He had worried for some time that Amanda was suffering for lack of a mother's influence. He had tried to compensate by letting her spend time with her maternal grandmother, until he became aware that Babette was spoiling her hopelessly.

He thought he understood his mother-in-law's motives. Having lost her daughter, she was afraid of losing Amanda, too. Bryce hadn't been able to make her see that being overly indulgent wouldn't help.

When Babette and Lyle Monroe learned that he was taking Amanda away from Nuee, they had acted as if he was taking their child away instead of their granddaughter. Provoked by their example, Amanda had accused him of ruining her life. She still had bouts of difficult behavior, too many for his peace of mind sometimes. He hoped that by removing her from her grandparents' influence, he would eventually make her understand that his decision had been for her good.

The dance ended and he thanked Elaine. On impulse, he asked, "Would you like some champagne?"

Under her mask she looked flushed, whether with the dancing, or at his offer, he didn't know. Had she expected him to desert her the moment the music stopped? He wasn't proud of having considered the idea.

"Champagne would be lovely, thank you."

He signaled to a passing waiter and lifted two flutes from his tray, gave one to her and toasted her with his own. "Thank you for your patience." It was more than he deserved.

She drank the toast without comment. "Will I see you again?"

He couldn't bring himself to promise anything while his gaze kept being pulled on invisible strings to where Giselle sat among her admirers.

Among a crowd of glittering people, she seemed to glow. Everything about her, from her crowned head to her slippered feet, shone with a brilliance that threatened to dazzle him. The mask prevented him from seeing all of her face but he had seen her picture often enough to know that her skin was flawless and porcelain toned, her opalescent gaze deep enough for a man to drown in.

He felt desire stirring, and warning bells rang in his brain. It didn't escape him that her lack of availability might be the reason he felt so strongly attracted to her. Coward, he told himself. Fixating on a woman he couldn't have was one way to avoid getting back into a game he had sworn he had given up two years before.

He hauled in a deep breath and opened his mouth to say something noncommittal to Elaine, but she spoke first. "It's almost midnight. I should see if the princess needs me for anything." She replaced the champagne glass on a waiter's tray. "Thanks for the dance."

Bryce inclined his head in agreement. "Thank *you*, Elaine. I'll see you around the castle."

But she was already weaving her way through the crowd to Giselle's side. He wasn't sure she'd heard him.

Elaine was exactly the sort of woman he should be interested in, he told himself. She was attractive, with a good sense of humor and the patience of a saint to put up with his inattention tonight, and she was obviously interested in *him*. She had even shown an interest in Amanda. What more did he need?

Fireworks, that's what. Candlelit dinners. Nights on satin sheets. The whole romantic ball of wax. The kind he'd known with Yvette, when they were starry-eyed with the wonder of love and the joy of their beautiful girl child.

At first they hadn't known anything was wrong, blaming the demands of a young child on Yvette's constant feeling of lethargy. When it persisted, she'd consulted doctor after doctor, being referred to one specialist after another. None could say with certainty why stray proteins were cluttering up her blood, and what it meant.

Not that a precise diagnosis would have made much difference. Over the years, despite valiant efforts at treatment, she had grown progressively weaker until she had begged him to make the doctors stop trying. Contrarily, once they did, she had rallied, giving him a glimmer of hope that she might recover against all odds.

When she started to spiral down again, he had sought out alternative therapies, from vitamin treatments to people who could supposedly heal by touch, anything and everything. For a short time her condition would seem to improve, only to continue once more on her inexorable downward path.

Even then, they had managed to snatch happiness from despair. Yvette had never been one for self-pity, and she had loved romance. He remembered bringing her a single Carramer orchid, a perfect specimen in a vivid cerulean hue that reflected her eyes. They had filled with tears of pleasure at the sight of the bloom.

At an earlier, happier time, they had picnicked with

Amanda in the rain forest on the slopes of Mount Mayat, not far from the Nuee Trail, where young riders pitted themselves against the mountain in a rite of passage to adulthood.

Watching a group of riders set out, Yvette had spoken of her dream to one day ride the trail as a family. He wasn't sure if anyone else had done that, and his excitement had quickened at the prospect. Not of conquering the mountain, but of sharing the adventure with the two most important people in his world.

Amanda had taken her first steps that day, he recalled, his mouth curving in nostalgia. The moment had been as much a rite of passage for her as riding the trail had been for the teenagers. He could still see his golden child pushing herself to her feet on the blanket and stumbling toward her mother, her baby eyes wide with astonishment at her own achievement.

That night he and Yvette had celebrated the milestone with a truly spectacular lovemaking, afterward wondering if they had created a brother or sister for Amanda. He had enjoyed ten magical years with Yvette, filling them with laughter and romance in spite of everything, because they had been determined to make it so.

After that, how could he settle for less?

The long and the short of it was, he couldn't. He didn't want to. The pain accompanying the memories was too sharp. Unthinkable to put himself through it a second time.

A pang gripped him. How had he gone from thinking about a mother for Amanda, to dreaming of romance, and being gripped by needs so strong he could practically taste them? Not because of Elaine, he knew. There was only one woman in the ballroom capable of making him feel like this, and she didn't even know she had done it.

He suspected that Princess Giselle would be horrified at his thinking. She had her own romantic agenda, and he wasn't part of it. In spite of the rumors about her and Robert Gaudet, Bryce had caught her disapproving reaction at hearing that she could only become Keeper of the Castle if she was married. Much as she obviously coveted the job, the princess didn't strike him as a woman who could be forced into anything.

It didn't stop him from wanting her.

Giselle's equerry rose from a deep curtsy. "It's almost midnight, Your Highness. I came to see if there's anything you need."

"Very thoughtful of you, but there's nothing for the moment. Have you enjoyed the ball?"

"I've had a great time. From the talk around me, this is the best Spring Ball ever."

"I'm glad to hear it."

She saw Elaine's glance go to her bandaged foot. "I realize it hasn't been fun for you, but…"

"It's all right, Elaine. I may not have been on the dance floor but I've talked my head off tonight." With the ease of long practice she stifled a yawn before anyone saw her. "Speaking of dancing, you seemed to enjoy the last waltz."

She saw her assistant color under the mask. "I had a fascinating partner. He wouldn't give me a single clue to his identity."

Me neither, Giselle thought, stifling her disappointment along with another yawn. She had hoped Elaine might have learned something about her mystery man.

He wasn't *her* mystery man, she reminded herself. He was either a friend of Maxim's or Eduard's, or a castle employee and she would have her answer as soon as the masks came off. No mystery about him.

"He did say he's new to the castle," Elaine volunteered.

All Giselle had to do was access the castle's security files and find out who had been given clearance to attend tonight's ball. Why hadn't she thought of it before? She could eliminate the guests she knew by sight, and those who had, contrary to custom, told her their names. She had been assisting her brother to administer the Merrisand Trust since she was twenty-one. Few names on the guest list would be totally unfamiliar to her.

"He has a ten-year-old daughter, but I'm willing to bet he isn't married," Elaine said.

Annoyed to feel a sudden sharpening of interest, Giselle asked, "What makes you think so?"

"He told me he's out of practice at dancing, and he came to the ball alone."

She told herself she was only interested for her equerry's sake, not her own. She had known Elaine since they were both teenagers, so they were as close to being friends as Giselle's position allowed. She didn't want to see the other woman get hurt.

"His partner may have stayed at home with their child," the princess suggested, not liking the agitation that accompanied this idea.

Elaine chewed her lip. "It could explain why he didn't seem eager to see me again, although I dropped a few hints. Not even to meet when the masks come off, so he can find out what I look like. Perhaps you're right, he already has a partner."

"Perhaps." To her frustration, Giselle found out she didn't want to be right for once.

"Did you speak to Prince Maxim and the Marquis about becoming Keeper of the Castle?" Elaine asked.

They had talked about the job as Elaine was helping Giselle to organize the ball. "I spoke to them. They agree I'm well qualified, but the charter is iron-clad. An unmarried woman can't hold the position."

Elaine made a sound of annoyance. "Can't you petition Prince Gabriel? As the governor of Taures, your father should be able to decree that the requirement is inequitable in this day and age. Men don't have to be married to hold the job."

Wishing she could stamp her damaged foot, Giselle nodded agreement. "You're missing the point. My father *does* know it's inequitable, but it suits my parents to have me in such a cleft stick."

"Because they see the position as an inducement to get you to marry?"

"Precisely."

"What about Robert Gaudet? The whole province would love it if their princess married the most eligible man in the kingdom."

"I don't intend ordering my life to entertain the kingdom," Giselle said sharply, then lowered her voice, aware of the other guests within earshot. "Robert is handsome and charming. I enjoy his company. I just don't see myself marrying him."

"Not even if it allows you to become Keeper?"

Giselle gave her attendant a sour look. "You sound like my parents. You'd think they'd be concerned about welcoming an actor into the royal family. Thespians are hardly known for their fidelity."

Elaine nodded. "Your parents probably feel that

the decision should depend on what's most important to you.''

Easier said than done, Giselle thought. The Keeper's position was important to her as a matter of simple justice. By doing the job for the last few years she had earned the recognition.

It wasn't only status she wanted but the right to put into practice some of her own ideas for the castle's future development. She and Maxim didn't always see eye to eye on what should be done. Invariably his will prevailed. Only when she held an equal position would her opinions carry the same weight.

Her mother had tried to assure her that she could achieve as much or more if she became the power behind the throne, but Giselle disdained such an antiquated notion. She knew Robert would love the title of prince, but he had his own stellar career. He didn't want to be involved in the affairs of the castle. So why should she have to ally herself with him in order to do the job in her own right?

Elaine leaned closer. ''Of course, the right man might make you feel differently.''

The idea struck so close to the heart of Giselle's thinking that she almost sprang from her chair. Only a hint of pain from her foot when she put pressure on it kept her seated. ''The tabloids seem to think Robert is the right man.''

''But you don't.''

Elaine knew her too well to pose it as a question. She alone knew that Giselle had asked Robert to go to America without her so she could consider the future of their relationship. In fact, she had already done so, but Robert had asked her to think it over while he was gone. Giselle didn't expect the time apart to make any difference. The spark simply wasn't there.

If she needed any reminding, she had only to consider her response to the mystery man. Now *there* was a spark. If it had glowed any brighter, she would have gone up in flames. His very touch had been enough to set her heart racing. Yet she didn't know his real name or anything about him. She only knew he had made her feel utterly alive and desirable.

Would she feel the same once the masks came off? As it was, she could make him into any man she wanted. Her dream lover, her Prince Charming. The mystery might be what made him seem so enticing. Somehow, she doubted it. Something in him had called to her soul like a voice in her mind, promising the earth if only she was open to possibilities.

Excitement shivered through her. She was probably letting the fantasy mood of the ball affect her more than it should, but for once she felt like indulging herself. She wanted to meet him, to stare into his eyes and discover if the spell was really there, or existed only in her mind.

And she wanted to do it on her feet.

"Please fetch me my walking cane," she told Elaine on impulse.

Her equerry looked startled. "I thought you didn't want to use it tonight."

"I've changed my mind. Hurry, it will be midnight in a few minutes."

The woman did as bidden, returning promptly with the cane the doctor had prescribed for Giselle's use until she could manage unaided. The princess looked at it in distaste. The sedan chair held far more appeal, but that would mean involving her bodyguards, and their presence was hardly conducive to the scene she had in mind.

Carefully she rose to her feet. To her surprise, her foot hurt only a little more than when she was seated, even when she put all her weight on it. She was definitely improving. Not wanting to undo the doctor's good work, she let the cane support her as she moved among her guests.

She had thought she had done her duty and spoken to absolutely everyone by now, but there were still people who wanted to congratulate her on her progress. All she was doing was walking, for pity's sake. Babies did it every day. She tried not to let her impatience show as she responded to the well-wishers in her slow circuit of the ballroom.

Her heart picked up speed as she scanned the room. Midnight was only seconds away and some people were already reaching to undo their masks. The orchestra struck up a bright tune and someone began a countdown. Her gaze became frantic. Where was he?

He was tall enough to stand out from the crowd, so she should have no difficulty picking him out. A wide-shouldered man in a dark suit had her heart double-timing until he turned around and she recognized him as a teacher from the castle school where she lectured in royal history.

Three. Two. One.

With a happy crescendo, the orchestra played into the moment. Laughter bubbled around her as faces were revealed, some expected, some obviously causing surprise. Nowhere could she see her mystery man. He had vanished as if into her imagination.

''There you are.''

Maxim stepped in front of her, his mask dangling

from his fingers. Reaching out, he unfastened hers and looped it over his hand. She wanted to wrench it back to hide her features from his searching gaze.

It was too late. "You don't look very happy for a woman who will soon be the toast of Merrisand. Thanks to your hard work and planning, this year's ball looks like it will break all fund-raising records for the trust."

"I'm delighted of course," she managed to say.

"I knew it was too soon for you to be walking. You're in pain, aren't you?"

Only if you counted the ache in her heart. "I'm fine," she insisted. She wanted to ask her brother if he knew what had become of the man who had offered her his arm at the start of the ball, but that would be far too revealing. They might be grown up, but her brother wasn't above teasing her as if they were still children, and she didn't think she could stand being teased about this.

She felt as if something precious had been offered then snatched away. She didn't know his name or what he looked like. Why had he left before midnight? He might at least have dropped a shoe so she would have some way to start looking for him. But this wasn't a fairy tale, and he—not she—was the quarry this time.

As soon as she could, she would go through the guest list name by name. Whatever it took. For now she would blame curiosity for the desire flaring incandescently through her. Only curiosity, nothing more.

Nothing she would allow herself, anyway.

Chapter Three

"That's all for today. Class dismissed."

The children streamed out of the classroom, bowing or curtsying as they passed her. Acknowledging them with a smile, Giselle stood up. It was great to do so without pain, and without having to depend on that wretched walking stick.

It was propped by her desk, but she could now move around the classroom unaided. By working at her physiotherapy exercises, she should be able to discard the stick altogether in a few more days.

The sessions had been tedious, only relieved by thinking about her mystery man. She still didn't know who he was, having been too busy catching up on the backlog of work to investigate. A substitute teacher had taken over her class while she was in Taures City, and Max had handled the most pressing of her royal duties, but many tasks had piled up in her absence.

Then as soon as she managed to find some time for herself, a virus had crashed the network of computers serving the executive offices, leaving her unable to access the staff files. She had been assured the problem would be fixed today, so she would have an answer soon.

Why was an answer so important? She hadn't even danced with him. And felt irritated knowing how much she had wanted to. As he escorted her around the ballroom, he had felt strong and dependable. She could easily imagine how his arms would feel if they came all the way around her.

Annoyance flashed through her like quicksilver. He was a phantom, most likely of her imagination. At least the strength and beauty of him. Without the mask and in broad daylight, his charms would probably have vanished. Besides, she had more pressing concerns right here.

Only a few children remained in the room when she said, "Amanda, may I see you for a moment, please?"

The child looked alarmed, then her expression blanked as it had too often when Giselle called on her during the lesson. It didn't only happen during the princess's class, she had learned by talking to the other teachers. They were all concerned that Amanda Laws wasn't settling in at school as well as she should be.

According to her file, the child had transferred here two months ago from a rural school on Nuee, where her performance had been exemplary. Not surprisingly, her grades had suffered after she lost her mother two years ago, but not to the extent that was becoming evident at Merrisand.

The school counselor had suggested that Giselle ask Amanda's father to bring the child to see her. The princess's commitments at the castle only allowed her to teach two classes a week, so on her last visit to the school she had sent the child home with a note for her father. Neither Giselle nor the counselor had received a response.

The princess frowned at the children hovering in the doorway, their curiosity burningly evident. At her stern look they scattered, leaving her alone with Amanda, who looked as if she wished she could follow their example.

"Please sit down," the princess urged.

Amanda perched on the very edge of the chair beside Giselle's desk, her hands clenched in her lap. Giselle hitched her hip on to the corner of the desk and softened her expression. "What did your father say when he received my note?"

The child's shoulders lifted and fell. "I don't know."

No title or other courtesy? "You did take it to him?"

"I left it for him."

"Your Highness." When Amanda looked at her in stubborn silence, Giselle said, "You can call me Miss Giselle if it's more comfortable for you." And less intimidating, Giselle knew.

Still no response.

The princess leaned closer. "Amanda, are you happy at Merrisand?"

She was startled when the child crammed her hand to her mouth, leaped to her feet and fled from the room.

Thinking hard, Giselle sat for a few minutes before reaching a decision. Not only was the child *not* happy at the castle, her father evidently took less interest than he should in her welfare. This would have to be addressed. She should probably allow the school counselor to handle the problem, but the woman wasn't at school today, and Giselle felt compelled to act now.

She spoke to her bodyguard about Amanda's flight, and he radioed security to look for her and make sure she got home safely. Amanda wouldn't appreciate the fuss, but Giselle wasn't about to leave the child to her own devices in her present state of mind.

If she'd thought it would help, she would have gone after her herself, but she felt she could do more good by talking to the child's father.

The deer park was outside the walls of the castle, extending into the forest bordering the castle to the north. The controller's residence was close to the castle boundary.

Normally she would have enjoyed walking there, but mindful of her healing foot, she took her car, distantly aware of her bodyguard's car falling in behind hers at a discreet distance as soon as she left the castle grounds.

She pulled in a steadying breath and looked around. The native sun deer were the most beautiful and delicate of their species and made driving between the pastures a positive pleasure. If she hadn't been so intent on her mission, she would have taken her time, enjoying the sight of the compact stags, with their impressive antlers, scattered amongst the herds of pretty, white-spotted females.

Some of the hinds had calves at foot, she noticed. Unlike many deer, they had no defined breeding season, so there were usually a few young deer gamboling around the pastures.

These were not all sun deer, of course. Most of the farmed stock were Mayat, providing a valuable source of venison meat that was now one of Carramer's most valuable exports. She didn't like to think of the beautiful creatures being so used, but neither was she a vegetarian, and meat had to come from somewhere.

She consoled herself that purebred sun deer were also raised at the park and released back into the forests to supplement the wild herds. Carramer's faunal emblem was in no danger.

Unlike the child whose father she was about to meet. Her brother had engaged the new controller while she was at Taures, so she had yet to meet the man, but had heard her attendants gossiping that he was a formidable specimen indeed.

He wasn't the only one, she thought, lifting her chin. She might not be Keeper of the Castle in name, but she was in every other way that counted, and the deer park itself was part of her own inheritance. In addition, Maxim usually entrusted her with decisions about the staff, and that included the controller of the deer park, who would have been engaged under contract.

A contract she could use as leverage to make him deal with his duty as Amanda's father.

She hoped it wouldn't come to that, of course. First she would try sweet reason. But since the man hadn't had the courtesy to respond to a note from the princess, she had little hope that a personal appeal would make much difference.

He wasn't in his office at the handsome stone residence when she arrived. A surprised housekeeper offered to send someone to fetch him. When this offer was declined, the woman informed Giselle that she would find him supervising the weaning of the season's new calves.

Should she take her walking stick or not? Giselle looked at the uneven ground and reluctantly took the cane with her. She didn't want to set back her recovery, and if the controller was as formidable as his reputation, she could always use the stick to bring him to heel, she thought grimly.

Her bodyguard wasn't enthusiastic about waiting for her at the car, but for Amanda's sake she wanted to meet the child's father on her own. She followed the housekeeper's directions to a complex of yards and laneways designed for the safe handling of the herds.

Deer could jump considerable heights, so the fences were higher than cattle would need, and those leading to the handling yards were shielded with hessian to prevent the deer from seeing through them. Unfortunately they also denied her a clear view of the controller's whereabouts.

Coming to a junction, she debated the way to go. Before she could decide, a man barreled toward her from around a corner, head down in thought, his stride long and purposeful. He didn't seem to realize she was there until she put out her arm to prevent him from slamming into her. Only her walking stick kept her from being bowled over.

Her free hand closed around muscle like solid rock.

He lifted his head, meeting her gaze full on. ''What in the devil…''

Her heart almost stopped. She would know those limitless blue eyes anywhere. It was him, her mystery man. He wore dusty black jeans and a gray checked shirt, with a black cowboy hat shading his face, but even without the evening dress, she would have recognized his lithe movements.

Without the black mask, his features were staggering. Hard-planed, tan from long hours spent outdoors. His nose was aquiline and slightly uneven as if from being broken some time in his youth, adding to an effect of rugged masculinity.

When he'd escorted her around the ballroom, his solid body and impressive build had given her the impression of an indomitable man. Added to the snap of power she saw in his clear blue eyes, she mentally added, a dangerous man.

Living a fairly sheltered life, she found the hint of danger exciting, even as it sent a shiver of apprehension along her spine. Here was a man not easily impressed by her position. He looked as if he expected people to earn his loyalty. Although having earned it, you would have it for life, she suspected.

Mentally she shook herself free of the spell like a puppy shedding water. At the ball he had talked about having a daughter. Amanda? If he was Amanda's father, he had some explaining to do.

"I take it you're the new controller?" she said, sure that he could be no one else.

He nodded tautly, not quite a bow, she noticed. She had a feeling he didn't readily bend his stiff neck to anyone. "Bryce Laws at your service, Your Highness."

The greeting was civil enough, deferential even. So why did she hear a challenge in it? "Not 'Clark' today?" she asked.

His gaze flashed fire. "He'd be out of his element here."

As are you, she read into his statement, telling herself she was foolish to read rejection into a simple response. Bryce certainly looked to be in his element, far more than he had done at the ball, she concluded.

She wasn't aware of speaking the thought until she murmured, "Pity."

His expression hardened. "'Clark' was a fantasy creation for one night. He did his job and now he's gone."

She couldn't believe it. Didn't want to? The man who had approached her so boldly at the ball, talked with her as an equal, given her his arm so she could meet her guests on her feet, couldn't be a fantasy.

He was before her in the flesh. And yet he wasn't. Being able to see all of his face should have made him more real to her. He was, if possible, more handsome than she had imagined under the mask, but somehow more unreachable.

This was crazy, she told herself. She had come to confront him about his neglect of his daughter, not to find a Prince Charming who existed only in her mind. That was the stuff of fairy tales. This was reality, and Amanda needed her help.

Determinedly she slid into what her brother called "princess mode." Being born royal had given her plenty of practice at hiding her feelings. No matter whether she was distressed, excited or bored out of her mind, she could usually conceal the truth under a serene royal mask. She did so now, although she was surprised how hard it was to do.

"I need a meeting with you, Mr. Laws," she said firmly.

He looked surprised. "Isn't management of the deer park Prince Maxim's province?"

She might have known he would prefer to deal with

her brother. Too bad, he was going to have to put up with her. "The park actually belongs to me. But what we need to discuss doesn't concern the park."

He gestured around them, although she could see nothing beyond the hessian barriers. "We're in the middle of weaning the current season's calves. I'd be happy to come to the castle for a meeting if you like."

At a more convenient time, she read into his words. Not accustomed to having her concerns dismissed out of hand, she felt herself bristle. "Are the deer offspring more important than your own?"

His attention hooked, he straightened. "Is something wrong with Amanda?"

The flash of concern she saw in his expression was too strong to be faked. For a moment she was confused. Surely a man who didn't care about his child shouldn't look so alarmed at the hint of something amiss with her.

"She's all right, but she ran off when I tried to talk to her. I sent the castle security people after her, and they'll bring her home shortly. She won't come to any harm in the castle grounds, and she can't go beyond them without one of my people seeing her."

The worry in his gaze changed to outright panic, quickly shuttered. Her confusion notched higher. If he was so plainly worried about his daughter, why hadn't he responded to her note?

He took her arm. "We'd better go back to the house."

She glanced at the hand on hers, telling herself the sudden, fast beating of her heart was due to surprise at being touched so familiarly. Apart from her attendants and doctors, almost no one touched her without permission.

He saw the look. "What?" Then realized and removed his hand from her arm. "Sorry, Your Highness. I suppose touching a princess is taboo at Merrisand."

He didn't sound sorry, as much as annoyed at being sidetracked, she noticed. He was already heading back the way she had come. She had to quicken her steps to keep up. "As you must have noticed at the ball, there are no taboos as such, but protocol does require a little less…intimacy."

Wrong word, she knew as soon as she saw his gaze brighten. "Must be a tough life if a friendly touch is considered intimate, Your Highness."

Her effort to match his long strides made her a little breathless. Or so she explained it to herself. "I wouldn't know."

Without slowing down, he glanced at her sideways. "Because you've never known any other life?"

"I was born in a castle."

"Here at Merrisand?"

She shook her head. "At the family residence in Taures."

That would be Taures Palace, he concluded, knowing he was distracting himself from worrying about Amanda. The princess was right. As long as his daughter was within the castle grounds, she was safe. All the same, he'd be a lot happier when she was home again.

Giselle's father, Prince Gabriel, might be the governor of the province, but Bryce would bet he'd feel the same way if his daughter were missing. Bryce had never met the prince, but Bryce's father had supplied the first successful crosses of Mayat deer to the royal estate in Taures. According to his father, the prince was a good man zipped into a royal suit so tight it was a wonder he could still breathe. Giselle's mother, Princess Marie, was said to be even more of a stickler for protocol.

With parents like those, Giselle's upbringing must have been stiflingly royal, he thought. She couldn't have had much experience of the ordinary pleasures between a man and a woman, if she confused a casual touch with intimacy. How would she cope if he showed her the real thing?

Now, where had that thought come from? Distracting himself from worrying about Amanda was one thing, but letting himself think of the princess in any personal way was a recipe for disaster. Hadn't he experienced enough heartbreak to last him a lifetime?

It didn't stop him from inhaling the sweet scent of Giselle's perfume as she hurried to keep up with him. Or thinking of how delicate she looked alongside his strength. Her fragility called to him, demanding his protection. He tried telling himself he only felt that way because of her rank, and his own tendency to protect those smaller than himself, a custom drummed into him by his father from an early age.

At the ball, Bryce had rationalized his behavior the same way, assuring himself he had spoken to the princess out of compassion, when everyone else was keeping a respectful distance. Even through her mask, he had sensed her loneliness and the frustration of having her movements restricted.

They weren't restricted now, he noted. Hardly using the walking stick at all, she moved with lithe grace, the legacy of years of deportment lessons, no doubt. He had never seen such a straight spine outside of the military. Even when slightly out of breath as she was now, she carried herself with regal elegance. He wondered what it would take to make her unbend.

At the thought, he felt long-neglected needs stirring within him. For the second time, he imagined how she would look with her hair freed from its classic chignon, tumbling in a riot of curls a man could run his fingers through. He envisioned her eyes brightening and her slender body trembling as he showed her the real meaning of intimacy.

It wasn't going to happen. She was a princess and he was in her service, nothing more. At least nothing he would permit himself. Once they found Amanda and he got to the bottom of what was bothering his child, he'd make sure he dealt with Prince Maxim about everything else.

He wished she would tell him what was on her mind instead of making him wait until they reached the house. As with the princess herself, he had to make an effort to stop his imagination from working overtime.

The problem was probably some small thing, like unfinished homework. If it had been anything serious, surely he would have known. Before he arrived, the deer park had been run by the assistant controller for a few weeks and things had become a little slack. Bryce hadn't had as much time to spend with Amanda as he liked, but that would change.

"Amanda told me you teach a history class at her school," he said, hoping to prompt a revelation.

The princess inclined her head in agreement. "She's a talented student, at least according to the records from her last school on Nuee."

He shot her a sharp glance. "You don't agree?"

"I haven't had a chance to find out yet. None of her teachers have."

They had reached the house. He held the door for her and she stepped inside. He was sure she didn't miss the signs of their recent arrival, the boxes still unpacked and the books in piles on the floor.

Two months wasn't all that recent, but he would get to the rest of the unpacking, he told himself. The housekeeper had offered to help, but he had assured her he could manage. The truth was, he was no more certain than Amanda that this was where they belonged. Had he put off settling in because it meant admitting that they were here to stay? Maybe he'd inadvertently communicated his restlessness to his daughter, fueling her unhappiness.

Where else were they to go? By selling Eden Valley he had burned his bridges. He could have lived out of a hotel, but Amanda deserved a real home. For her sake he would start making this place into one, he promised himself. First he had to make sure she was all right.

At least the living and dining rooms were presentable, if a bit impersonal. The lovely antique rosewood furniture had been here when they arrived. A few personal touches wouldn't hurt, he thought, seeing the living room through the princess's eyes as he showed her into it.

If she noticed, she was too well schooled in hiding her reaction as she seated herself gracefully on a tapestry-covered sofa. Her back made no connection with the back of the sofa, he noticed, trying not to gulp at the way her skirt fell away in graceful folds, exposing her long legs when she crossed them.

Again he felt the urge to shatter her composure but

bit down on the temptation and tried to emulate her steadiness. "Would you like coffee? Or would you prefer tea?" What did princesses drink, anyway, and where the blazes was his daughter?

"Water would be fine, thank you."

Mrs. Gray hovered anxiously in the doorway, and was delighted to be given something she could do for her princess.

Bryce barely contained his impatience until she had served the water, curtsied and left. Then he leaned forward in his chair. "I know Amanda still has some settling in to do at the castle school, but I wasn't aware of any other problem, Your Highness."

"Not even after reading my note?"

He looked perplexed, then angry. "I didn't receive any note."

A tiny frown marred her serene expression. "She told me she left it for you."

"Not that she gave it to me?"

Giselle obviously hadn't considered the distinction. "Where would she have 'left' it?"

"Probably the one place I've been to busy to touch for several days—my desk."

He uncoiled from the chair and left the room, returning a few minutes later with a note in handwriting Giselle recognized as her own. "It was there, under a pile of forms waiting to be filled out," he said, sounding slightly embarrassed.

Her cool nod made him feel as if he was the one in her class, not Amanda. Damn it, she made him feel that he had been neglecting his daughter, when Amanda was his first consideration in everything, including the move to Merrisand.

''Perhaps you'd be kind enough to read it now,'' she suggested.

Decision time. Either he was autonomous here, or he wasn't. The forms on his desk included an agreed adjustment period when either side could still rescind his contract.

''I'd prefer to hear it from you, Your Highness.'' With that, he crumpled the princess's note in his hand.

Chapter Four

He managed to make her title sound anything but deferential, she noticed. She kept the anger out of her expression. This was about Amanda's welfare, not her own feelings. If only she weren't awash with so many of them, it would be easier to maintain focus, she thought.

Now that she knew Bryce was her mystery man, she should feel content. Mystery solved. Instead she found herself wondering if he was as gentle as he was strong. If he could make a woman's heart beat as fast when he held her as he did with a look.

Why he should have such a disturbing effect on her state of mind. And not just her mind. Her entire being vibrated with awareness of him. No other man had ever made her feel so conscious of her own womanhood.

She blinked. Pulled herself back to the moment. First and foremost she was a princess, in command of any situation including this one. So why did she feel so at sea? "Amanda isn't paying attention in class," she stated.

His expression cleared and a slight smile turned up the corners of his mouth. The effect was of the sun coming out.

"Children never pay attention in class, at least not willingly. When you were a child, didn't you ever look out the classroom window on a bright summer day and dream yourself somewhere else? I know I did."

"I didn't have a classroom, at least not in the sense you mean. I had tutors for most of my education, until it became the norm for members of the royal family to attend regular schools."

"Then how can you know what it's like for my child, especially when you only see her for a few hours a week?"

Keep calm, she ordered herself. Don't react. It was hard when every part of her wanted to rant and rave at him to make him see what was under his nose. His child was desperately unhappy.

"This isn't just childish inattention," she insisted. "I agree that my official duties let me spend only part of each week with the children, but I've conferred with her other teachers and they agree that Amanda isn't settling in at Merrisand." Her glance swept the room, somehow penetrating the wall to include the still-packed boxes. Was Amanda the only one having trouble settling in?

His smile faded, replaced with a concern that tugged at her heart. "I ask every day, but she doesn't say much about school, except to complain that history lessons stink."

Amusement played around her mouth. "History isn't her strong suit?"

"There are other subjects she prefers."

"Such as?"

She saw him think for a moment. "She's passionate about art. I've promised to set up a place where she can do her sketching soon."

When he had time, she added mentally. "I gather the deer park is taking up a lot of your time." She tried not to make it sound like an accusation, even though it felt like one to her. Maybe it should.

He heard it, too, she saw when he frowned. "Pulling the park into shape is a big job. From Prince Maxim, I gather you haven't had a controller for some time."

"Deer require skilled management. Since your predecessor retired through ill health, it hasn't been easy finding the right replacement. The other staff are the best at their jobs, but without a strong hand at the helm, things were bound to slip."

He leaned forward, resting his forearms on his knees. "Even so, it's no excuse for not being aware that something's wrong with my own daughter."

Giselle gave a regal nod, concealing her surprise at the admission. She hadn't expected him to agree so readily. Had she been at risk of misjudging him? "It can't be easy raising her alone," she conceded.

"Harder than I ever imagined. Not only having to be both parents to her, but also knowing how much she's missing, not having a mother. How much her mother is missing, too. Every milestone in Amanda's life is a painful reminder."

"To Amanda, too," the princess said.

His breath gusted out. "Yes."

"What was her life like before you came to Merrisand?" She wasn't fishing, she told herself, remembering his words to her at the ball. She was merely trying to understand his child.

He seemed to struggle with himself, then she saw his shoulders square and he became matter-of-fact. Probably the only way he could deal with the memories. "We were happy, at least until Yvette became ill. Even during the long months after that, there were moments of joy. My wife insisted on it."

Giselle suspected that Bryce had been answering as much for himself as for his daughter. "And Amanda?"

"She was a normal, healthy child. We tried not to burden her with too many adult concerns. She knew her mother was seriously ill, but we made sure she still had a childhood. At Eden Valley, she rode her horse with her friends and went out sketching almost every day. That's one of her drawings."

Giselle's gaze went to the only picture hanging in pride of place over the fireplace. Other framed pictures were propped against the wall, ready to be dealt with eventually. She went to inspect the drawing of a sun deer and its calf against a forest backdrop.

One didn't grow up among some of the most valuable paintings and etchings in the kingdom without gaining an appreciation of art. Especially when Giselle shared Amanda's enthusiasm for sketching. The princess's practiced eye told her the painting was naive but filled with promise.

She turned back to Bryce. "I think she has real talent."

He nodded agreement. "Yet she hasn't drawn anything since we got here."

"You didn't find that worrying?"

"I thought being in a new place, she had too many other distractions, or that she might be growing out of her old hobby. It's happened before. When she was five she was determined to be a ballerina."

Giselle, too, remembered a time when she had dreamed of being a ballerina. Taking ballet lessons had been part of her education, and she had been good at it. Unfortunately a princess didn't have the luxury of such a career choice.

"The drawing was the only hobby that lasted," he went on. "When she stopped, I should have seen it as a pointer to her state of mind."

"Children can be very adept at hiding their true feelings." Now who was speaking on her own account? Her parents had never known how much she wanted to dance.

He joined her in front of the painting. "All the same, I have to get to the bottom of this."

"That's why I'm here. I tried to talk to her after class, but as soon as I asked if she was happy here, she jumped up and ran away from me."

Forgetting himself, he clamped his hands over her upper arms, swinging her around to face him. Anger erupted in his gaze. "What kind of school is it, that she could be driven to run away from you?"

She quailed inwardly but kept her outward cool, knowing she would be equally distraught in his place. "Her state of mind is what we need to establish. In the meantime, you should calm yourself. She can't go anywhere beyond the castle walls. She'll be brought home as soon as she's found."

She hoped she was right. Rather a lot of time had passed since Amanda ran out of the classroom. Giselle's conscience twinged as she realized she had allowed her response to Bryce to distract her from what should have been her main concern.

Even now it wasn't easy to keep her mind on anything else, when he stood so close. His fingers bit into her arms. She would probably have bruises there tomorrow. She couldn't make herself care. All she could see was his wide, mobile mouth and wonder how it would feel if he lowered it to hers.

She swallowed hard, saw him do the same, making her wonder if he felt the same pull of attraction. He released her and she made an effort not to massage her upper arms, not wanting to reveal how much his touch had affected her.

"My apologies, Princess," he said, sounding distracted. "You probably have a bookful of rules against being manhandled."

None that she could drag to mind at this moment. Not when he made "princess' sound like an endearment.

"It's forgotten," she said, not sure how honestly. "This is a difficult situation. One can't help becoming overwrought."

The sound of a car pulling up outside brought his head up and she saw hope mingled with fear spring into his gaze. She felt slightly ashamed of her earlier belief that he was a neglectful father. No man who looked as ragged as he did now could be accused of not caring.

Moments later the housekeeper showed in Kevin Jordan of the R.P.D. and a mutinous-looking Amanda Laws. Kevin impassively reported to the princess, and received her assent to return to his normal duties.

Giselle shot a covert glance at Bryce. He looked

torn between wanting to take his child in his arms, and fury that she had put him through such anxiety.

The child didn't bother to hide her resentment at being escorted home, and looked even less pleased to see the princess. "What's she doing here?"

"Princess Giselle was kind enough to be concerned about your welfare. You will show her the proper respect," Bryce snapped, the anxiety winning for the moment.

Amanda's lower lip quivered, but she remained silent.

"Amanda?" Bryce prompted in a tone that brooked no argument.

"Thank you for worrying about me, Your Highness," Amanda said in a singsong voice of obligation.

Bryce relaxed fractionally. "And nothing like this will happen again."

"Nothing like this will happen again," she parroted dutifully.

Giselle felt her heart squeeze with concern for the child, but kept her expression carefully neutral, not wanting to undermine Bryce. "I'm glad to hear it. But I would like to know why you ran away when I asked whether you're happy at Merrisand."

"Because I'm not. I want to go back to Eden Valley." Intercepting a warning look from Bryce, the child added, "Your Highness."

Progress of a sort. "As I told you this afternoon, you are welcome to call me Miss Giselle. Lots of the children do. I know how hard it can be surviving in a strange place, away from your friends."

Amanda's dubious look raked her. "How do you know what it's like, Miss Giselle. You're a princess."

"Being royal doesn't exempt me from having feelings. When I was about your age, the monarch decided all the royal children should go to normal schools.''

She had the child's attention, she saw. ''Didn't you go to school before that?''

''I had private tutors who came to my father's palace. So when I went to a real school for the first time, I didn't know how anything worked, where to go or what to do.''

Bryce was also intrigued, she could tell. Although she was accustomed to sizing people up at a glance, she found him difficult to read, but the softening in his gaze encouraged her. She took Amanda's hands. So small and cool. ''I felt much the same way I imagine you're feeling now,'' she added.

Amanda didn't pull away. ''Did you run away?''

''I wanted to, but princesses have to put a good face on things, so I had to stay and learn how to fit in.''

''I'll never fit in here,'' Amanda denied.

Giselle thought she heard a fraction less defiance in her tone. ''Perhaps you need to give it more time. A couple of months isn't long.'' She took a deep breath. ''Your father tells me you like to sketch. I do, too, and I sometimes invite a group of students to a sketching group at the castle. Would you like to be included?''

Amanda hesitated, plainly torn between her anger and her passion for drawing. Passion won. ''Yes please, if it's all right with you, Daddy.''

Bryce met the child's gaze levelly. ''It's going to depend on how well you behave over the next few days, young lady. Do I have your word there'll be no more running away?''

"Yes, Daddy."

He held out his arms to her and the child went into them, the warmth of the gesture spearing Giselle with longing. Then he held Amanda slightly away from him. "Very well. Next time Princess Giselle holds her sketching group, you can join them. What do you say?"

His reward was a slightly breathless, "Thank you, Your Highness." Amanda even managed a wobbly curtsy before her father dispatched her to her room to do her homework.

As soon as the door closed behind her, Bryce fired a suspicious glance at Giselle. "How often does your sketching group meet?"

Nerves climbed into her throat. He had the strangest effect on her, as if he could see all the way to her soul. She told herself it was nonsense, but he was far too perceptive for her comfort.

He didn't look pleased about her inventiveness. "As you've obviously worked out, I hatched the idea just now. I thought it would give Amanda something to look forward to. How did you guess?"

"It wasn't hard, Princess. You're already up to your ears in royal duties. You teach at the school twice a week, and you're gunning for the job of Keeper. It doesn't leave a lot of time for teaching schoolgirls how to draw."

"All the same, I've had the idea in mind for some time."

He stood up and jammed his hands into his pockets. "With respect, Your Highness, I'm perfectly capable of looking after my own daughter."

She swallowed hard, unused to feeling so overwhelmed by anyone. Lord, he was big. And plainly furious with her for usurping what he saw as his role, although she hadn't intended any criticism. Did he doubt his adequacy as a parent? Was that why he was, to her mind, overreacting?

"That isn't why I suggested the group," she said quietly, although her heart was racing. "Amanda has talent worth fostering. I would hate to see it dissipated through unhappiness, when I can do something to remedy this situation. I have a teaching degree as well as my masters' in business, but I'm hardly qualified to advise you as a parent."

He nodded acknowledgment of the fact. "Then you have my permission to include her in your group."

She had to bite her tongue to avoid pointing out who outranked whom here. He didn't seem in a mood to appreciate being reminded of protocol right now. If he ever would be.

For a commoner, he was remarkably comfortable around royalty, she decided. In her experience, she had to work at putting most people at ease when they met her for the first time. Bryce had no such difficulty. No wonder she found him so refreshing.

Careful, she cautioned herself. She still hadn't fully resolved things between her and Robert. And even if she had, Bryce had shown no interest in her as a woman. Better not to start reading more into this than was warranted.

He paused in front of her, balancing easily on the balls of his feet like the captain on the deck of his ship. His ship, she noted. There was no trace of the tenant farmer about him. He might be in the castle's employ, but he would always be his own man, she suspected. She saw his gaze narrow. "Tell me, Your

Highness, do you take this much interest in every one of your subjects?"

She had been asking herself the same question without reaching any helpful answer. Or was she afraid to look at the real reason: that she was attracted to Bryce in spite of all the reasons that she shouldn't be?

When his identity had been a mystery, she had rationalized her interest as curiosity. Now that she knew who he was, the feeling should go away. Instead, it gnawed at her, making her want to act in uncharacteristic and, her parents would say, unroyal ways.

Her mother was bound to have a rule against getting involved with a man like Bryce.

So why did she feel as if she wanted to, against all odds?

Her family approved of Robert Gaudet, she reminded herself. The people approved of Robert, seeing a romance between the star and the princess as the ultimate fairy tale. They were all anticipating a happy ending. Except that she knew it could never be like that between them. Robert was handsome, talented, strong; her match in every way except the one she craved, love.

Was she a fool to want to be swept off her feet? Robert and her parents all thought so. Maybe they were right. Within the family, her childhood nickname had been "Just So", because that's how she liked things. Was she expecting too much now?

Maybe romance was never "just so," at the start, anyway. She and Robert might grow into love, as her mother had patiently explained she had done with Giselle's father.

Irritated with herself, Giselle chased the thought

away. She had no business letting Bryce Laws put such ideas in her head.

"I take an interest in everything to do with the castle," she told him.

"Is that why you want to be Keeper?"

So you can meddle in everyone's affairs? She heard the question he didn't ask. "I'm not a control freak, if that's what you're thinking," she said sharply, not wanting him to see her that way.

His eyebrows lifted. "I wouldn't dream of suggesting such a thing, Your Highness."

Anger with him and herself made her snap, "Oh, for goodness' sake, call me Giselle, at least when we're alone."

He gave a slight bow. "With pleasure, Giselle."

She felt the ground shift beneath her. The way he said her name made it sound beautiful. As if he thought she was beautiful. She didn't permit many adults outside her family to use her given name. Wasn't sure why she did so now. Unless it was to hear him say it so seductively.

Something deep inside her purred in response.

"I want to become Keeper out of simple justice," she went on, trying to ignore the feeling. The need. "I'm already doing the job. There's no fairness in denying me the title just because an ancient charter says a woman has to be married to qualify."

He folded his arms over his broad chest. "Doesn't an ancient charter give you your position in the first place?"

The question had her blinking in surprise. He was referring to the centuries-old Charter of Succession, the basis of the de Marigny family's right to rule Carramer. "As a princess, you mean? I suppose it does."

"I take it you don't object to being bound by that?"

"You're telling me I can't have it both ways." Her brother had already said much the same thing. She let her tone tell Bryce how little she thought of the notion.

"But it doesn't stop you wanting to."

How well he understood her at short acquaintance. "Do you think I should give up my dream of becoming Keeper?" she demanded.

He prowled to a side table and picked up a Lladró figurine of a deer, examining it without really seeing it, she suspected. "Dreams are wonderful, Giselle. But we can't always make them into reality."

If they could, he wouldn't be living at Merrisand and Giselle would never have met him. Perhaps it would have been better that way. She had trouble convincing herself.

Chapter Five

Thinking of Bryce became a bad habit over the next few days. Images of him popped into Giselle's mind at the most unlikely moments, when she lay half-awake before her lady-in-waiting brought her an early-morning cup of tea; while having her hair dressed for a state occasion or as now, when she was trying to work.

Usually she had no trouble focusing her attention on the monthly reports of her heads of department. Well, technically Maxim's heads of department, but he hadn't chaired a meeting of the Keeper's Committee in eighteen months. He had his hands full administering the Merrisand Trust and the castle's art and curatorial departments. Everything else he left to Giselle.

"Next up is the report of the Master of the Household, rather a long one, I'm afraid," her equerry, Elaine, said as she placed a thick file on the desk.

"It is the largest and busiest in the castle," Giselle

agreed. She felt as if she was awakening from a trance. As a serving officer in the Carramer Royal Navy, Elaine had excellent instincts. Giselle hoped her equerry hadn't noticed that her princess had signed the reports of the Armorer and the Proclamations Officer without absorbing a word of their contents.

What was the matter with her? Normally she took a keen interest in the affairs of every one of the departments. Some of their titles might sound antiquated, but their activities were nothing if not up to date. Where once the Proclamations Office might have nailed parchments to a church door for all to read, these days they were more likely to design the castle's Internet web site, or answer e-mails from children all over the world. And far from being concerned with swords and suits of armor, the Armorer headed the Royal Protection Detail, responsible for the castle's state-of-the-art security protocols.

She made an effort to listen intelligently as Elaine summarized the household report, but could summon little enthusiasm for domestic matters and catering arrangements. She would read the reports more thoroughly before the next committee meeting, she promised herself.

When she wasn't so distracted.

Elaine didn't seem to notice. "Last but not least, the Master of the Royal Estate."

Giselle felt her attention sharpen involuntarily. As well as the stables, gardens and forests of Merrisand, this department included the deer park. Since the park was outside the castle walls, it had become customary for the controller to report directly to the Keeper's

Committee, rather than through the appropriate department head.

She leafed through Bryce's report on the nutrition, water and health needs of the deer herds, finding herself smiling at supplemental feed tables and stocking rates. Not because such matters fascinated her, but because she could imagine how enthusiastic he would be about compiling reports.

He would be more interested in the practice than the theory, she guessed, picturing him as a hunt-and-peck typist who probably muttered to himself about bureaucratic interference as he worked. But his report was meticulous and detailed.

When she said so, the equerry nodded. "Our new controller seems to know what he's doing. I heard on the grapevine that he's the mystery man I danced with at the ball."

A pang shot through Giselle. "You don't normally pay attention to castle gossip."

Elaine's eyes twinkled. "Only when there's a man involved. And a widower, so I was told."

"We've met," Giselle said dryly. "His daughter is in my history class."

"Naturally, you needed a parent-teacher meeting with him as soon as possible."

About to caution Elaine not to overstep herself, Giselle bit her tongue. Since choosing Elaine as her equerry, Giselle had encouraged an air of informality between them. Not only did it get the work done faster, it made Giselle feel like a real person instead of a figurehead.

Now she had to wonder why she felt so defensive about a teasing comment. She made herself smile.

"As it happens, you're right. I called on him a few days ago at the park."

"And?"

"And nothing. We discussed his daughter's schooling and I offered to tutor her in sketching, since it's an interest we share."

If Elaine had drawn any conclusions about Giselle's sudden urge to set up the sketching group that the two of them had discussed earlier in the week, she was wise enough to keep them to herself. "Pity," she said now. "If he's as impressive at other activities as he is on the dance floor, I can think of lots of things to discuss with him other than his child's education."

So could Giselle. "Nevertheless, that's what we talked about. Since Amanda is having difficulty settling into life at Merrisand, I invited her to the sketch group this afternoon, so she'll feel part of the castle family."

"Of course." Elaine looked pointedly at her boss's hands.

Unconsciously Giselle was stroking the pages of Bryce's report. She stopped abruptly, feeling herself grow hot. Despite assuring Elaine that her concern was for the family's well-being, Giselle knew Bryce was in her thoughts far too much lately. Twice she had been tempted to call him with some trivial question, but had stopped herself before he got the wrong idea about her interest in him.

She told herself he was a new employee. It was natural that as the de facto Keeper, she should get to know him better. The thought was less convincing than it should have been.

The light on her private line flashed. With a murmured apology to Elaine, she picked up the receiver.

A resonant masculine voice said, "Hello, darling, I hope I'm not interrupting any crucial affairs of state."

Trying not to think of the male voice she would have preferred to hear, Giselle guiltily injected a pleased note into her tone. "Hello, Robert. We're only working on the monthly reports."

"We'll finish these later," the princess mouthed to Elaine, who stood up and quietly left the office.

"How are things in America?" Giselle asked Robert. Her gaze lingered on Bryce's signature on his report. It was bold and flourishing, sloping slightly to the right, the loops spilling over the computer printout as if he had signed the document in haste, glad to get it finished.

No doubt he had been, if her impression of him was accurate.

She pulled her attention back to Robert Gaudet, who was talking about his new film project. "American enthusiasm is amazing. I could have bankrolled the production twice over, and I'm on the way to tying up a distribution deal."

"Congratulations."

There was a pause. "Aren't you going to tell me you've missed me, Elle?"

"I thought the whole point of the separation was to miss you."

"You don't sound as if you have," he observed a little petulantly.

She traced Bryce's signature with her fingernail, unable to imagine him being petulant about anything. He would come out and say whatever was on his mind. "You know how I feel, Robert. If you hadn't asked me to wait until after you completed your current deal, we would have made our situation public by now.''

''The deal was just an excuse. I asked you to wait so you'd think things over and realize you're making a mistake.''

If she was, it was hers to make. Robert was a good friend, but the separation had confirmed her suspicion that he would never be anything more. He was right, she *hadn't* missed him. And surely she should have done if their relationship had any meaning?

It had begun well enough at a royal command performance she had attended in Solano with her cousin, Prince Lorne, and his family, two years ago. Afterward when they went backstage to meet the performers, Robert had been the only cast member not looking overawed about being presented to royalty.

He had held her hand a few seconds longer than protocol demanded, tightening his grip so she couldn't easily extricate herself. When she leaned toward him to exchange a few polite words, he had pulled her closer, whispering in her ear that she looked ravishing and wasn't it a pity there were all these other people around?

Sheer surprise had made her blush warmly, prompting the media to speculate about what exactly the actor had said to the princess. A newspaper even ran a contest so readers could offer their own suggestions, she recalled uncomfortably.

A few days later he had sent her tickets to his private box at the opening of a new play. She had known her acceptance and attendance at a celebratory dinner afterward would fuel rumors about the two of them, but she hadn't expected quite the furor that erupted.

She knew her behavior wasn't always what the

public expected. Too headstrong and opinionated, she rarely fitted anyone's image of a fairy-tale princess. So becoming the focus of approving headlines for once made a pleasant change.

Robert had managed to charm the royal family as thoroughly as he'd charmed his public, she thought. The monarch himself had told her what a handsome couple they made. Max's reaction had been equally warm. She couldn't blame them, since she hadn't shared any of her later misgivings about Robert with her family, leaving them to accept the relationship at face value.

Even the approval rating for the monarchy in general had notched a few points higher as people followed the glamour couple's progress in the media.

Now she had the unenviable task of making it known that she and Robert had parted on amicable terms. The royal wedding everyone anticipated so eagerly wasn't going to happen.

The blame would fall squarely on her, she expected. And she probably deserved it. Robert wasn't the one complaining about the lack of sparks between them. Like her family, he thought they were ideally matched, calling her Elle as a sweet—if to her, irritatingly blatant—public sign of affection. Their careers were complementary, their fame equally stellar. They coped as well apart as together, although Robert assured her he preferred the latter.

She wasn't so sure. Although she chided herself for being cynical, she had noticed how his production company had prospered since he became linked to a member of the royal family. She didn't begrudge him his success. The son of a teacher and a housepainter, he had worked hard to get where he was. But she wanted more from a relationship than being his stepping-stone to greater things.

"I think the mistake is in continuing a relationship that isn't based on love," she said.

"You know I love you. I hoped you would come to feel the same way in time."

So had she. "I know, but it isn't going to happen."

"It pains me to hear it, Elle. I really thought we had something going. Can we at least remain friends?"

The defeat she heard in his voice almost made her regret her decision. But he was a skilled actor. How could she be sure he wasn't acting now? "Of course," she agreed. "I'm sorry things worked out this way."

"For pity's sake, don't compound this by apologizing. What we had was wonderful while it lasted. I'd hate to think you were apologizing for any of it."

"I'm not. I just need you to understand why I can't be what you want." What anybody wanted, it seemed. Not the rest of her family, nor the Carramer people. The only person who had looked on her with unconditional approval lately had been Bryce, when his devilish gaze had claimed hers at the ball.

She shivered, remembering. He had looked at her with such desire that her breath caught. If he had stayed until midnight for the unmasking, who knew where the night might have led?

Nowhere, she told herself angrily. He was not only a member of her staff, he was plainly still grieving for his wife. If he'd been the least bit interested in Giselle, he wouldn't have left the ball without so much as a by-your-leave.

Having sent Robert to America only days before

the ball, knowing it was over between them, she had seen what she wanted to see. What she needed to see. A man who thought she was beautiful and desirable for her own sake. Not for him, the ostentatious use of a nickname to let the world know how close they were. Bryce had used her given name like a caress, devoting his attention to her needs rather than his own.

Bryce might not be interested in her, but he had set what she had decided would be her gold standard for how she wanted to be treated in the future, she resolved inwardly.

"I have one last favor to ask," Robert continued. "I'd like your permission to use the deer park as a location in my new film."

Had they still been together, he wouldn't have had to ask, she knew. Conscience made her say, "Yes, of course. Is there anything else I can do to help?"

"Marry me," he said huskily.

She kept her tone light, but regret at knowing she had disappointed him came through anyway. "Anything but that."

"Then I guess there's nothing. I have a couple of people already scouting locations near Merrisand. I'll tell them to contact your equerry and make arrangements to look at where we might film in the park."

"It will be my pleasure." Her parting gift to him as well.

To her relief he made no further attempt to change her mind, and said goodbye as if they were, indeed, friends. After he hung up, she sat lost in thought for a long time before pulling herself together and buzzing Elaine to continue their meeting.

* * *

"You don't have to drive me to the castle for the sketching group. I'm not a baby," Amanda protested. "I promised I wouldn't run off again, and I won't."

Bryce ruffled her hair. "I accept your word, chicken. But I want to assure myself that everything is as it should be. I have to go to the castle in any case."

Not strictly true, he thought as Amanda flounced off to get her sketching materials. He had already submitted his monthly report on the state of the deer park, although he had nearly torn his hair out trying to be diplomatic about the improvements he felt were needed. Never having had much patience with bureaucracy, he found the royal kind even more trying. Why couldn't he simply pick up the phone and tell Prince Maxim what he thought, man to man? In the end, Bryce had stuck to the facts. As reports went, it was probably dry as dust, but at least he hadn't offended anybody. Yet.

The Keeper's Committee didn't meet until later in the week, another waste of time. There was so much he wanted to do at the park to bring it up to scratch that sitting in meetings wasn't going to achieve. When in Rome, he reminded himself. At the same time, he knew that buying his own land and being his own master couldn't happen soon enough.

The questions he wanted answered could wait until the meeting. And Amanda was right. At ten, she was old enough to take herself to the princess's sketching group. So why was he so keen to take her there himself?

Because it was the princess's sketching group.

He hadn't seen Giselle since her visit to the park, but it didn't mean he hadn't thought about her. Every time he was around the gentle sun deer hinds, seeing the morning light glint off their golden coats, he was reminded of Giselle's lustrous coloring. She was as delicately formed as the deer, with an inner core of strength he admired.

In her position she could have instructed one of the teachers to talk to him about Amanda. Instead, Giselle had preferred to approach him herself. Seeing what she thought was his neglect of his daughter, she hadn't hesitated to confront him. If he *had* been letting Amanda down, he had no doubt the princess would have berated him soundly.

He wondered if the people of Merrisand realized what a remarkable woman they had in her. She deserved to become Keeper of the Castle. As far as he could tell, she was already doing the job. Insisting that a woman be married before she could hold the title, when the same rule didn't apply to a man, was inexcusable in his opinion. So what if ancient custom dictated the rules? If ancient rules couldn't be changed, his grandfather's country would still be ruled by a British monarch, and slavery would be acceptable.

He told himself he was getting hot under the collar because he hated injustice in any form. It had nothing to do with Giselle's beauty or charm, and certainly not because he wanted to get involved with her. He didn't want to get involved with anyone, especially not a princess who was, as far as he knew, on the verge of marrying her film star.

Amanda came back, her expression sulky. "I hope we don't have to sit in a stuffy room and draw some dorky bowl of fruit or something."

He hooked his leather jacket over his shoulder with

one finger. "If you do, I trust you'll remember your manners and treat the princess with respect."

Amanda nodded agreement, but as they walked to the car he heard her mutter, "I thought this was supposed to be fun."

Ten minutes later, a footman showed him and Amanda into an airy, plant-filled conservatory where, Bryce was informed, the group was to meet. A few easels, stools, paper and sketching materials had been set out among the hothouse plants. Evidently it was to be a small group.

Soon afterward, three chattering schoolgirls joined them, acknowledging Amanda and Bryce with cool smiles but no friendly overtures. When Bryce saw her avert her eyes and pretend not to care, his heart bled for his child.

Resolutely he strolled over to the girls. "I'm Bryce Laws, Amanda's father. We haven't been introduced yet."

"Tara Lehua," said the first, adding emphatically, "*Lady* Tara Lehua."

Strike her off the list, Bryce thought, although he nodded. The second girl gave a faint smile. "I'm Alexie Mondrian. My mother's in the Proclamations Office," she said in a voice he had to strain to catch.

Her problem was shyness, not snobbishness like Lady Lehua, he concluded. He turned to the third girl, who volunteered, "I'm Mary Jo Downey. I'm from San Francisco, but we live here now, after my dad joined the R.P.D. three months ago."

Another newcomer. He breathed a silent prayer of thanks. "Perhaps you could show Amanda the ropes, since she's new here." Behind him, he could almost hear his daughter's groan of dismay. Too bad. She wasn't going to remain an outsider one second longer than he could help.

"Sure," Mary Jo said. "You can sit beside me, Amanda. But there are no ropes. This is the first time Princess Giselle has held the group. We had to be recommended by our art teacher at the castle school. How did you get included?"

Amanda looked down, then up again. "The princess invited me herself."

Even Lady Lehua looked impressed. "You must be really good," Mary Jo enthused. "Maybe you'll be the one showing me stuff."

As the two girls' heads drifted closer together, Bryce removed himself from the circle and settled against a wall at the back of the conservatory, feeling satisfied with his handiwork.

He was thinking about leaving, when the princess swept into the room. He got to his feet, seeing the girls do the same. Giselle nodded acknowledgment and gestured for them to sit. She looked relaxed in narrow-legged black pants and a shirt the color of ripe corn. Her hair was caught at her nape by an amber clasp, a few curls escaping to spill around her face. She carried a drawing tablet under one arm.

He found himself wishing he possessed some of Amanda's talent so he could sketch the princess as she looked now, almost as young as her charges and utterly charming.

While she briefed the girls on how the group would operate, he feasted his eyes on her loveliness. How could a woman handle the responsibilities she had either inherited or chosen and look so untouched?

He amused himself by imagining they were alone in the green, fragrant setting. The orchids and exotic ferns made a fitting backdrop for her beauty. The lightly perfumed air teased his senses, prompting flights of fantasy such as how it would feel to touch his lips to hers and hold her slight body in a gentle embrace.

She was like one of her own hothouse flowers, to be treated with great care, although that would mean fighting his inclinations. Keeping his embrace gentle when his masculine instincts demanded he take what he desired wouldn't be easy. Sometimes it was hell being civilized.

His body stirred powerfully, reminding him that this was only a fantasy.

"Since Amanda's father has decided to stay and observe, why don't we warm up with a quick sketch of him."

He saw his daughter roll her eyes and was tempted to do the same. Standing inconspicuously at the back was one thing. Having the princess fix her full attention on him was quite another. He began to straighten, to summon a polite refusal.

"Hold your position," she said, her tone freezing him in place. Not the royal command in it, but the interest in him. A subject, not a man, he thought, irritated with her and himself. What difference did it make, unless he wanted her to see him as a man?

Giselle wasn't sure what had made her single out Bryce as her subject. She had planned to have the students sketch one of the spectacular orchids in full bloom. But something about his pose, relaxed yet so completely masculine, had piqued her interest.

After the girls shuffled their easels around, there came the scrape of charcoal on paper. "Don't try to draw Amanda's father," she instructed, echoing her own beloved art teacher of years before. "Simply draw what you see—a long body leaning against the wall, one leg bracing his body at an angle, the other crossed over it at the ankle, arms folded loosely over his chest. You aren't drawing a whole figure. You're drawing light and shadow, lines and angles, whatever is in front of you. See only the part you're drawing and its relationship to the next part. Don't censor yourself. Simply draw."

Her own pen was streaking across her sketch pad. She hadn't expected to see Bryce here and her body had reacted of its own accord, her pulse picking up speed and heat rising through her like a tide. She couldn't fault him for acting as a concerned father in bringing Amanda to the group, but his presence complicated Giselle's feelings.

Another axiom from her old teacher sprang to her mind. "Don't tell me about your feelings, draw them." Giselle had been angry with the teacher for criticizing a sketch she'd been especially happy about. He'd urged her to draw her anger, pouring her fury onto the page. The result had been one of her best works.

Looking down at the finished sketch of Bryce, her heartbeat snagged. She had drawn her feelings, but the sketch didn't reveal annoyance, or even objectivity.

She looked up and found him watching her as intensely as if she were his subject. A flush swept through her as she dealt with the message her fingers had delivered to a mind unwilling to hear. You could hate Bryce Laws or you could love him, but being objective wasn't an option.

Chapter Six

As a footman escorted them back to the car after the class, Bryce regarded his daughter's flushed face and sparkling eyes with pleasure. How had the princess known so exactly what Amanda needed?

The rolled-up cartridge paper under her arm told its own story. After overcoming her anger at Giselle for involving Bryce in the group, and with her father for complying, Amanda had sketched an astonishing likeness of him. He planned to frame it, although he felt certain that the sketch would look amateurish in future, as her talent matured.

"You had fun today, didn't you?" he asked.

Wrong thing to say, he saw as soon as her face drained of its vivacity. Why couldn't he keep his fool mouth shut? "You saw how *Lady* Lehua treated me? I get the same deal at school every day."

"Mary Jo was friendly enough," he pointed out.

"You didn't give her much choice. I ended up looking like a try-hard."

"Now just a minute," he began, then saw the quiver in her set jaw. Maybe she was right. He was the one trying too hard, both to be a good parent and to make her like Merrisand, so he could feel okay about bringing her here. He washed the censure out of his voice. "You're right, you don't have to like it here if you don't want to. All you have to do is make it work until we can have our own place again." It wouldn't be long, he vowed silently.

"We had our own place."

Patience, he counseled himself. "We had a place owned by the family company, with Grandpa holding the majority vote, making sure we all knew it. Next time, our votes will be the only ones that count."

A faint glimmer of a smile lit her features. "Promise?"

He took her free hand, feeling gratified that she didn't tug free. "Promise."

The sketch of Bryce lay on Giselle's desk as she worked in her office a few days later, taunting her with its message of an attraction she didn't want to feel. Yet looking at the tender way she had transferred his likeness to paper, she couldn't deny it either.

Careful, she warned herself. She was on the rebound, her emotions roller-coaster unsteady. Although she hadn't been in love with Robert, she had enjoyed their time together. Enjoyed being part of a charmed couple. Probably the reason she had let it go on too long.

I'm like Pavlov's dog, she thought. Reacting to approval by wanting more. Before meeting Robert, she hadn't cared about her public image, until the headlines began to portray her in a flattering light. She

was surprised she had found the strength to break off
the relationship, given the chorus of disapproval that
was sure to follow. She knew she would have to make
some kind of official announcement soon, but she
wasn't looking forward to being the black-sheep princess once again.

Should she have married Robert as everyone
wanted her to do? Doing so would have qualified her
for the Keeper's job. Robert would have continued
making his films and she would have had what she
wanted. They probably wouldn't have had to see that
much of one another. Her family would tell her it was
a sensible arrangement. Royal marriages were frequently made for reasons other than love. Was she a
complete fool for wanting more?

Raised voices outside her door made her look up.
A moment later Elaine came in. Giselle understood
why her equerry hadn't used the intercom when she
saw Bryce looming behind Elaine.

The equerry sounded uncharacteristically flustered.
''Mr. Laws would like a word with you, Your Highness.''

This morning she had appointments coming out of
her ears, but the next one wasn't for twenty minutes.
She could spare him that much time. Surprised how
much she wanted to, she said, ''I have a few minutes.
Send Mr. Laws in, and see that we aren't disturbed.''
She could rely on Elaine to signal her on the intercom
if time got away from her, as she suspected it might
with him.

Elaine looked surprised, but stood aside to let
Bryce pass, then closed the door, leaving them alone.
The princess motioned him to a seat, but he ignored

it and towered over her desk. "Thank you, but this won't take long, Your Highness."

"I thought we agreed my name is Giselle."

"That was before you let your boyfriend's film crew crawl all over the deer park without having the grace to check with me first."

Bryce's presence in the sketching class had driven her promise to Robert out of her mind. "I meant to tell you," she said, then reminded herself who was in charge here. "The park is within my portfolio. I have no obligation to consult you before authorizing access to it."

He planted both hands palms down on her desk, bringing his face close enough for the faint fragrance of his leathery aftershave lotion to provoke her senses. "Actually, you do, Princess. My clear understanding from Prince Maxim was that I would have complete autonomy over the park. I wouldn't have accepted anything less."

No, you wouldn't, she thought. Her palms felt damp and she had to work to keep her breathing even. "I'm sure by autonomy, Max means where the deer are concerned. The park is part of Merrisand and comes under royal jurisdiction."

Bryce's eyes flashed fire. "Then you'd better get yourself another controller."

She stood up, aware of her heart beating uncomfortably fast. She needed to meet him eye to eye. As soon as she was on her feet she was reminded how impossible that was. She would face him on her feet, anyway. Moving around the desk, she said, "May I remind you that you're under contract?"

"Remind all you like. Neither you nor the prince seem to have noticed I haven't actually signed it yet."

It was so unlike her to have missed such a critical detail, that she felt her hands start to tremble, and pressed them together. "Remiss of you," she said quietly, although inwardly she felt a shrill of anxiety. Not because they would have to find a replacement if he walked out, but because everything in her rejected the idea of letting him go.

His gaze caught and held hers. In his eyes she saw challenge and something more. An awareness of her that reflected her own feelings. Surely not. "Remiss of you and your brother," he amended.

"A verbal contract is still a contract."

He moved closer, holding his arms rigidly at his sides as if he was afraid of what he might do with them. She felt no fear for her safety, only the excitement of imagining those same arms holding her tightly.

"As you've probably heard, a verbal contract isn't worth the paper it's written on," he said, his voice dropping into a seductively low register.

The vibration of it traveled through her all the way to the soles of her feet. "You won't walk out."

"Try me."

Desperate to defuse the heated moment, she tried another angle. "Why is a visit from a film crew such a problem for you?"

"If you have to ask, then you know very little about deer farming. The pregnant hinds have to be kept calm and left alone as much as possible. They can easily be spooked into miscarrying. I don't even go into those fields, yet your boyfriend's people wandered right across the area, not caring what harm they could be doing."

"He isn't my boyfriend," she insisted, aware that she didn't want Bryce thinking he was.

He made a dismissive gesture. "Fiancé then. Does it matter?"

"It matters to me. Robert and I ended our relationship when he was in America."

She had to be imagining the sudden sharpening of interest in Bryce's gaze. She hadn't intended to tell anyone about the breakup until she decided how to make it public with the least repercussions for the royal family. Why had she wanted Bryce to know?

"And you felt so guilty about it, you gave him free run of the park."

How did he know? While they talked he had moved closer, and suddenly she became aware that his large frame was eating up her personal space. She caught her breath and said in her most regal tone, "You presume a great deal."

Bryce knew he was about to presume a lot more. Somehow he had known this moment would come from the time he set eyes on Giselle. He was so angry with her he wanted to shake her. Instead, he took one more fateful step closer and lifted his hands to run them experimentally down her arms. She shuddered but didn't summon her guards and order him dragged off to her dungeon, assuming she had one.

Today she wore a businesslike silk shirt in a fiery cerise color, with a short, tight navy linen skirt that revealed a long expanse of leg encased in the sheerest hose. On her feet were navy stilettos that still only brought her up to his shoulder. As he ran his hands slowly along her silk-clad arms, he felt his heart start to race. The shirt was buttoned almost to the neck. His fingers itched to play with the pearl buttons, to undo them one by one, exposing more of her porcelain skin.

He saw her drag in a ragged breath, feeling himself do the same. Keeping his gaze locked with hers, he slid a hand along her collarbone and up into the silky waterfall of her hair. The strands tangled around his fingers the way Giselle herself seemed to be tangling around his brain.

His insides tightened. "Where you're concerned, presuming is becoming a habit of mine," he said tightly.

She looked confused, as if nothing like this had ever happened to her before. "I have appointments," she said, sounding slightly desperate.

He knew exactly how she felt. "This is one of them. We just didn't know we were making it."

She let her head drop back, her eyes almost closing. What incredibly long lashes she had, he thought. He stroked one with a finger, making her open her eyes in astonishment. He felt himself drowning in the lambent depths.

One taste, he promised. One taste then he would walk out. He wasn't the type to subordinate himself to anyone. Maybe that's why he hadn't signed the contract, because subconsciously he knew it wasn't for him. Some men were team players and others were lone wolves. He felt the howl gather at the back of his throat.

Instead of howling, he kissed her, and the effect on him was almost the same.

Her lips were every bit as soft as they looked. The first sample made the blood rush to his head so fast he felt unsteady, and tightened his grip on her arms.

At night, lying in the controller's house, the silence

deep enough to touch, he'd dreamed of her, of this. She'd haunted his thoughts since the ball, and he'd known he would turn dream into reality one day. Perhaps not so soon. Or maybe not soon enough, he mused as warmth spread through him. Waiting for this moment had seemed like an eternity.

Giselle felt her head start to whirl. What on earth was she doing, letting him kiss her? She should step back, demand he remove his hands from her arms and remind him of her position. Remind herself.

She stayed where she was as heat swirled through her, pooling deep inside into a longing so fierce it was like pain. Her lips parted on a cry and he took it for the invitation it was, deepening the kiss until the blood sang in her veins.

As his lips took and took from her, she shivered with unmistakable pleasure. His hand moved from her arm to the back of her neck, massaging her nape under the prim collar of her shirt. Shivery sensations shook her. She felt anything but prim. She felt wild, wanton. Hungry. She'd been kissed before, but never like this. Never before like this.

For such a powerful man, he was surprisingly gentle, making her ache for what she felt sure he was capable of giving. She didn't want gentle. She wanted his primitive strength, his hardness against her softness.

She did something she hadn't known she was capable of doing. She began to seduce him, letting her mouth and hands show him how he made her feel. What she wanted. Oh, the wanting. She had never felt anything like it before.

He felt her response threaten his control. For a princess, she was a wild woman, returning his kiss—no, nothing as simple as returning it—demanding and urging until he wasn't sure who was seducing whom.

Her passion called to him, telling him here was a woman who could match him and then some. Heat tore through him at her touch, until his kiss became a dance of desire, a prelude to what he knew they would share in time. It was as inevitable as night following day.

Needing more and more closeness, he cupped her linen-clad rear and held her against him so she would know what she was doing to him. The skirt had ridden higher and her stocking tickled his palm, tempting him to explore even higher. Did she wear stockings or panty hose? Stockings, he hoped, imagining her peeling them off slowly for him, one at a time.

His throat became a desert, and he forced the image away. Being able to kiss her felt like a miracle. He knew he must not hope for more, despite the fire threatening to consume him.

She was relentless in her demands, pulling his head down until he couldn't stop himself from closing his teeth around the delicate flesh of her neck. He was careful not to do any damage, but he felt her tremble in his arms, and a soft sound that might have been a moan erupted in her throat.

The sound echoed in his mind, making him want to give her more. One day it might come to that. The way he felt now, the day would come soon, if he allowed it.

He couldn't, for both their sakes. She was a princess and deserved more than he had to give. However transcendent a physical experience might be, and Lord knew it would be, it wouldn't be enough. And he had nothing else to give her, not materially and certainly not emotionally.

All the same, it required every bit of self-discipline he possessed to drag his mouth away from hers. He saw her eyes fill with questions as he firmly lifted her hand from the back of his neck and tucked it between them, creating a space that felt like a chasm.

"This won't do. You're a princess."

"I'm still a woman."

He raked a hand through his hair. "You don't have to tell me that." It was as a woman that she had shaken him to his core. For a few heart-stopping minutes he had forgotten her rank, forgotten why he shouldn't kiss her, forgotten everything except how good she felt in his arms.

He had entertained wild thoughts of making love to her right here on her desk, until sanity returned. Now it had, he was stunned by how easily she had made him forget. "This won't do," he repeated.

She was panting and had to fight to slow her breathing, to regain control, before she could summon her voice. "I didn't know it could be like that."

He clasped his hands around hers, keeping them between their bodies. It was precious little space, but he didn't yet possess the will to move away. "Sometimes, there's a connection between two people. Surely you've heard of chemistry? That's all this is."

She swung her head in determined negation. "This is more than chemistry."

"No. You said yourself you've ended your relationship with Robert Gaudet. I've lost my wife. That makes us sitting ducks emotionally."

Was he right? She hated to think so, but he sounded so matter-of-fact it was tempting to believe her re-

sponse to him was only a result of emotional vulner-
ability. If not for her heart beating far too fast, and
the clamminess of her hands, not to mention an ache
in the pit of her stomach. She couldn't accept that
they meant nothing. She shook her head. "It's more
than that."

She saw bleakness invade his gaze. "Because you
want it to be. I have nothing to give you, Princess."

He had given her more in the last moments than
any other man had ever done. "You underestimate
yourself."

He shook his head. "I'm simply stating facts."

"Your facts."

"The only facts that make any difference. I'm your
employee. As soon as I have the resources, I'll be
gone from Merrisand. You'll remain here, doing your
royal duty, eventually marrying your own kind. It's
better if we forget what just happened, Your Highness."

So they were back to rank and title, she thought
bleakly. How could she forget the glorious way he
had made her feel? "Is that what you want?"

"It's what I have to want."

Not quite the same thing. It came to her that the
attraction could be all on her side. Was he trying to
find a face-saving way to say he didn't want her? She
could have made herself believe it, if not for the
shocking evidence of his arousal when he'd cupped
her against him.

He wanted her.

But she was a princess and wouldn't beg. If he
thought she was so shallow that she required riches
or a pedigree from her suitors, then he wasn't for her,
no matter how he made her feel.

Stepping away from him, she tidied her clothes and gathered her dignity around her as if the last few tumultuous moments hadn't happened. "We're agreed that this is forgotten, Mr. Laws," she said as regally as if her heart wasn't crazed with tiny cracks.

His face drained of color as though he hadn't expected her to take him at his word. "Princess...Giselle," he said, sounding anguished.

He couldn't have it both ways. She drew herself up. "Giselle is still acceptable between us. Is there anything else?"

This time he needed no mask to become unreadable to her. "Nothing."

"Then you are dismissed."

His eyes flashed molten fire, suggesting he would like to argue, to take back his demand that she forget what he had made her feel. For a giddy heartbeat she wished he would. If he then took what they both knew she wanted to give him, how could she prevent it? They would be bound together regardless of any stupid limitations he wanted to impose.

But he was stronger than that. The fire in his gaze flickered out, and he moved easily toward the door as if leaving was his own idea. It was, of course. She was fairly sure that, had he chosen not to go, no royal command could have shifted him. Only a certain rigidity in his posture suggested that leaving cost him anything at all.

She drew comfort from the idea, even if it was a product of wishful thinking. Another thought occurred to her. "Bryce, wait."

He turned back slowly. "Yes, Your Highness?"

Stop it, call me Giselle in that wonderful, seductive tone, she wanted to scream. Instead, she pulled in a steadying breath. When she was sure she could speak normally, she said, "I won't have the film people interfering with the orderly running of the deer park."

He seemed to search his mind for understanding, as though she had made him forget why he had come to her. Good. Why should her head be the only one spinning? She saw his expression clear as he retrieved the memory. "What do you propose?"

To avoid meeting his eyes, she fiddled with a gold desk set. "You may tell the film people that I have placed all visitors to the park under your authority. No one is excepted. It will be your decision as to where you let them go and what you permit them to do. Objections may be referred to my equerry."

She looked up as he inclined his head graciously. "Thank you, Your Highness."

He didn't sound grateful. He sounded as if she had done no more than he expected, she thought, irritation flaring. If she hadn't been made so conscious of her effect on him, she would have wondered if she had been manipulated into doing his bidding. He was more than capable. And she hated to think how willing she had been.

"Will there be anything else?" he asked, carefully matching her formality.

Nothing she was prepared to share with him.

Her intercom flashed, making her draw a sharp breath and remember where she was. Her next appointment was due, when all she really wanted was to sit and stare out the window, savoring the sensations Bryce had wrung from her.

There was no time, not for her, and definitely not for them. "No," she said heavily. "You may go."

As the door closed behind him, she knew that it was the last thing she had wanted him to do.

Chapter Seven

When Bryce got back to the park he wasted no time finding the movie people and laying down the rules. He even enjoyed it. The producer, a fussy man in his fifties, made it clear that he wasn't used to receiving less than red-carpet treatment and would complain to the executive producer, who happened to be Robert Gaudet. Bryce was surprised how much satisfaction he took in telling the man to go right ahead.

Making it clear he had the princess's backing to run things his way, he told them exactly where they could go and what they could do within the park. This wasn't Deerworld, and the deer weren't special-effects toys. They were valuable wild animals and too much stress could harm the stock, even kill them. He also pointed out that his staff would enforce the rules and eject anyone who flouted them. They could tell that to Gaudet, too.

Satisfied, he went back to more useful work.

It was late afternoon by the time he finished overseeing the feeding run and strategic placement of the mineral blocks needed to supplement the herd's diet, and headed home to shower and change. He had snatched a quick lunch on the job, and looked forward to spending some quality time with Amanda.

By the time he emerged feeling human again, she still hadn't returned. Frowning, he looked at his watch. She and Mary Jo were working on a project together after school, but she should have been home by now.

He called the school library, but two girls weren't there. However, the librarian had seen them go into the Youth Vocational Center in Merrisand Village, outside the castle wall.

Replacing the receiver, he felt another frown settle on his forehead. What were Amanda and her friend doing in a center for troubled teenagers? Was his daughter in some kind of trouble? She had promised not to run away again and he trusted her, but these days there was a gulf between them he couldn't seem to cross. Would she tell him if she had a problem?

He reached the center in record time and was directed to an office, where he found Amanda, her arms full of files. Mary Jo was on the floor sorting more folders. Amanda looked surprised to see him, as well she might.

"What are you doing here, Dad?"

He closed the door. "I was about to ask you the same thing. You told me you were working on a school project today."

She gestured with her free hand. "This *is* our project. Today we were studying the Merrisand Trust, and Miss Giselle assigned us to find out some ways the trust helps other children. They provide the funds for this center, so we asked if we could visit and see what they do here.''

From the floor, Mary Jo nodded. ''Mrs. Martin, the director, is really nice. She told us how the center teaches underprivileged teenagers how to do trades and crafts and stuff so they can get jobs and have a future. She was so helpful, we wanted to do something in return, so she let us help organize some files.''

The princess hadn't mentioned any of this. He hadn't given her much chance, he realized. He had been too busy kissing her and wishing they could do more. Heat raced through his veins like quicksilver until he subdued the recollection. What kind of father indulged his own raging hormones at his child's expense? Just as well he had regained his sanity in time.

He recalled the note Amanda was supposed to bring to him. ''Did the princess send a permission note home about this, for me to sign?''

His daughter shook her head. ''She meant for us to work in the library, but I thought this would be better, because of Mom and all.''

''Amanda says her mother used to work in a center like this,'' Mary Jo contributed.

He went cold from head to foot. He had been so busy blaming himself and the princess that he had overlooked the obvious. His daughter possessed half her mother's genes. Yvette had been a counselor at the local youth center on Nuee until she became too ill.

He and Yvette had met when she brought a group of teenagers to Eden Valley to learn about deer farming. He had been so taken with the petite beauty with the core of steel that he had asked her out. She had

accepted on condition that he allowed some of the
kids to gain work experience on the ranch. He would
have agreed to almost anything she wanted in order
to see her again, but her request made it too easy. He
had been glad to do it, and had kept up the involve-
ment until Yvette's illness had made it impossible.

Why wouldn't Amanda have inherited some of her
mother's passion?

"Where is Mrs. Martin now?" he asked gruffly.

"Getting a cup of coffee," Amanda said. "She'll
be back in a minute."

"When she comes back, would you like a ride
home?"

Amanda nodded. "Mary Jo's dad was going to take
me. Can she come with us?"

So Amanda no longer considered herself a try-hard,
and had a real friendship in the making. He sup-
pressed a smile. "Provided she clears it with her
dad."

"You're not mad at us for coming here?"

He might be mad at himself for not knowing what
was going on with his child. Mad at the princess for
being so beautiful and sexy that she drove his responsibilities out of his mind. But not at his daughter
for inheriting her mother's generosity of spirit. "I'm
proud of you," he said, and took the files from her,
setting them down so he could hug her to demonstrate
how pleased he was.

Too restless to sit down, Giselle prowled around
her brother's office, picking up objects and replacing
them without really seeing them. She saw him wince
as she tossed a priceless crystal paperweight from
hand to hand then replaced it on his desk.

Maxim reached over and pointedly moved the paperweight away from the edge. "I appealed to Lorne, but not even the monarch can overturn the terms of the charter. He's willing to put it to the people, but even if they agree, as I'm sure they would, the change can't take effect for five years and one day."

"I know," she conceded on an outrush of breath. She had always believed it was good that the charter had been designed to resist change. Except that the architects hadn't foreseen the emancipation of women from being their husbands' helpmeets, to a force in their own right. "Thank you for trying, anyway."

The prince linked his hands together on the desk. "For what it's worth, I think you'd do an excellent job as Keeper."

"I am doing it," she reminded him.

He gave her a wry smile. "I stand corrected. So why is the title so important?"

How could she explain her need to be her own person in at least one area of her life? As the eldest and a male, Max took precedence over her in everything. She might have the Keeper's responsibilities, but she wasn't really the Keeper and needed Max's support for all major decisions. He didn't readily withhold it, and frequently deferred to her judgment, but it rankled to have to ask.

The thought of having a husband take over where Max left off was too much. Was that why she had ended her relationship with Robert? He was cut from the same cloth as Maxim, and his celebrity status meant he was also used to having his wishes obeyed. As a member of the royal family and with a title bestowed on him on their marriage, he was likely to become even more controlling.

She would be relegated to a ceremonial role, or worse, a decorative one with no chance to stretch herself to her limits. By the time they had children, as she hoped to do one day, she would be a clone of her mother, subservient to her husband and stifled by protocol forever.

She gave a delicate shudder. ''Isn't it enough that it *is* important to me?''

''You could always change your mind and marry Robert.''

At the start of their meeting she had told Max about her decision. He hadn't been pleased that she hadn't consulted him, but he had appeared to accept it. She threw herself into a chair beside his desk. ''Give me a good reason why I should.''

''I can think of two. Robert loves you and the whole province expects the two of you to become engaged.''

In her opinion neither were good reasons, especially not the last one. ''Do you think I haven't considered that?''

''Have you thought how you're going to announce that the two of you have broken up?''

She crossed one slim leg over another, aligning them at a graceful angle until she remembered her mother's injunction, and defiantly uncrossed them. ''I've thought of little else for days. Why can't we be allowed a private life like everyone else?''

''Goes with the territory,'' he said philosophically. ''Rank has its privileges, but they come with a price.''

Sometimes more than she wanted to pay. She picked up the folder of notes she had brought and proceeded to discuss them with Maxim.

Work had always been her cure-all. But today it

seemed less satisfying than usual. While one part of her mind focused on the activities of the various departments, another part went off on its own quest.

She should be concerned about how best to announce her parting from Robert, but the memory of Bryce's kiss kept getting in the way. She blamed him for her distraction, although she knew it was unfair. He hadn't forced her into his arms or made her endure the press of his lips against hers. Remembering how eagerly she had taken whatever he gave and demanded more, she felt herself flush. Was it only forty-eight hours ago? It felt like a lifetime.

Her tongue skimmed over her lips now, her temper rising as she wondered why he had such a disturbing effect on her. He was as commanding as her brother, perhaps more. At least Max observed the basic courtesies. He didn't storm into her office and make demands as Bryce had done, without even the excuse of rank.

Bryce didn't need rank to be master of his life, she accepted. She had done some research, learning that the land he had sold before coming to Merrisand had belonged to a family company. His grandfather, who headed the company, had a reputation for running a tight ship. No ship could have two captains, so Bryce had allowed the land to be sold.

Not a man who would play second fiddle to anyone, princess or otherwise.

What was she thinking? She had let him kiss her out of curiosity. She had enjoyed it. How much hardly bore thinking about. But it had to end there. If he couldn't tolerate his grandfather's yoke, Bryce would never accept hers. He would want to command her, and that she would not allow. Max would say they could be a team, but every team needed a leader. As long as Bryce was around, she knew who it would be.

The intercom on Max's desk flashed. He glanced at her inquiringly. "Go ahead, I'm almost done," she said. She wasn't much use to him while her thoughts were in such turmoil.

He murmured a response to his equerry, then turned to her. "Robert Gaudet is waiting for you in your office."

"But he's in America."

"Not anymore. He flew in an hour ago, and wants to talk to you."

She didn't want to talk to him. "Everything we needed to say has been said."

Her brother gave her a supportive smile. "Evidently he doesn't think so."

She gathered her notes together. Shouldn't her heart be picking up speed at the thought of Robert waiting for her? Instead, the numbness she felt told her she had done the right thing. Why wouldn't he accept her decision?

"Because I don't think you've thought this through, Elle," he said when she confronted him with the question.

The Californian sun had topped up his elegant tan, so he looked handsome and prosperous. His full head of hair was brushed back apparently carelessly, and a faint sprinkling of gray at his temples gave him a distinguished, if slightly rakish, air, although she suspected the gray had the help of a clever stylist.

He wore a collarless white shirt over impeccably tailored charcoal pants, with a cream cashmere sweater slung around his shoulders, the sleeves looped in front. For almost a year she had been thrilled to have her name linked with his, had seriously thought about marrying him. Now she couldn't help thinking he looked what he was, a man to whom image was everything.

She placed the leather-bound file in her out tray for Elaine to deal with, and settled herself behind the desk. "On the contrary, I've given my decision a lot of thought."

He frowned. "You realize how this will look?"

"I'm willing to accept any blame."

"I'll still be the royal castoff for the rest of my life."

She was right, image was his main concern. She noted he hadn't said anything about her feelings. "You could always start a torrid new affair, and make me look like the castoff."

She had spoken in jest, but she saw him seriously consider the idea. "Or you could," he mused. "If I found you with another man, I would be the wronged party, wouldn't I?"

What would he say if she told him she *had* been in another man's arms only days before? "Can't we simply say it's over?" she asked, feeling tired. It didn't help that Robert was willing to let her reputation be dragged through the mud, as long as he came out on top.

Something akin to panic came into his eyes. "You don't understand. The backers of my new project think I'm about to become a prince of Carramer. Why do you think they were so eager to invest millions of dollars in my new film?"

"You had no right to tell them you had royal assent."

"I didn't tell them anything. They drew their own conclusions."

"But you didn't correct the impression that I support your production company."

"I believed you did."

Couldn't Robert hear himself? This was more like a business meeting than the ending of a relationship, she thought. At least she didn't have to worry about breaking his heart. "What do you want me to do?"

He leaned forward, resting his forearms on his knees and letting his head drop. If she hadn't known what was really bothering him, she would have felt much worse. He looked up. "Short of you having an affair so I look like the injured party, I can't think of anything that won't wreck my film before it gets off the ground."

"I could delay an announcement until your investors are securely under contract," she said, then quenched his quick flare of hope. "But I won't be a party to deception."

"Of course not, you're a princess."

"Isn't that my main value to you?"

The acid in her tone made him flinch. "I really care about you, Elle. Not only because of the film. We made a great couple."

Fantastic publicity value, she couldn't help thinking. His was a cynical world, and he was making her cynical too. She didn't much like herself this way. "We had some good times," she conceded and rose, wanting to have this over with. "I won't make anything public for a few more days. It's the best I can do."

He stood up, automatically posing as if a camera was on him. "You could also speak to that fool Max appointed to run the deer park. My producer called me in America to say he's making life impossible for my crew.''

She masked her anger with a brittle smile. ''Prince Maxim chose Bryce Laws for his expertise. Bryce is far from a fool. I gave him authority over your people for the good of the park.''

Robert's expression turned bleak. ''It really is over, isn't it? You've gone back into that royal shell I thought I'd cracked for good.'' He turned to leave, then spun back, his expression accusing. ''Is this Bryce character the reason you want to be rid of me?''

She drew herself up. ''He has nothing to do with us.''

''That isn't what I hear.''

''You've been a victim of gossip often enough not to believe everything you hear.'' Inside, she went cold. Had someone in the castle read too much into her encounters with Bryce? She glanced at where her sketch of him had lain on her desk for days. It was gone. She didn't recall putting it away, but she must have done. Just as well. The drawing was far too revealing for Robert to see.

Stiffly she offered the actor her hand, a vision of Bryce touching his lips to it filling her mind. ''Good-bye, Robert.''

He didn't touch her but ducked his head in a parody of a bow. ''Your Highness.''

When he walked out, she felt as drained as if she'd run a marathon.

She needed some air. Normally she would have saddled up her favorite riding horse and gone for a canter through the Great Park, but her foot was healing so well that she didn't want to risk a setback. A walk then.

She hadn't been conscious of heading for the deer park until her feet took her that way. A concealed path led to a locked gate, but she had a key. The path continued through a remnant of ancient forest behind the old castle wall, emerging at Home Park and continuing along the borders of the deer park.

Behind her she heard her bodyguard, Kevin Jordan, puffing slightly as he matched her brisk pace, and she slowed. As children she and Max had taken fiendish delight in moving as fast as they could, forcing their minders to jog to keep up. As adults they were more considerate.

She turned, catching Kevin's eye. "I won't be leaving the confines of the park. Would you have my car brought around to the controller's lodge and wait there until I'm ready to drive back?"

Walking both ways wouldn't have troubled her, but she didn't want to overtax her foot. Nor did she want anyone shadowing her every move. Sometimes, as now, she just needed some time to herself.

Kevin didn't look happy to leave her but was too well trained to argue. "I'll see to it immediately, Your Highness."

Left alone at last, she filled her lungs with the pine-scented air and continued down the path at a more relaxed pace. Watching the deer graze peacefully in the enclosures surrounding her, she felt her tension ebb. There was a good reason why they were thought to be the most beautiful of their kind. Their golden coats were marked with black stripes along their flanks, and drifts of white on their fronts and undersides.

The sight of a splay-legged six-week-old fawn grazing beside its mother made her wish she had brought her sketch pad. She moved carefully so they didn't react to her presence. They were notoriously timid and excitable, the reason Bryce had objected to the presence of the film crew. Unlike Robert's crew, she knew that stress could kill the deer.

Other than for a few workers going about their tasks in the distance, she was alone. She told herself she wasn't looking for Bryce and didn't care if their paths failed to cross.

She also believed in the Easter Bunny.

Fixing her gaze on the drifts of leaves beside the path, she became annoyed with herself. What good would it do if she did find him? He wasn't the man for her, if any man was. Should she resign herself to a spinster's life? At least she would be in control of her own future. Maybe she should leave Merrisand altogether and pursue a career as an art teacher in a university somewhere.

Tempting but impossible, she knew. She couldn't abandon her duty any more than she could stop being royal. Titles and privilege mattered less than blood. No matter where she went or what she did, she would remain a princess of Carramer in her heart. Robert hadn't understood. She wondered if any man ever could.

Chapter Eight

Bryce immediately recognized the royal standard fluttering on the hood of the car pulling up outside the controller's lodge. He allowed himself a smile of satisfaction. So he hadn't been the only one replaying their kiss over and over in his mind like a broken record. She hadn't been able to resist seeking him out.

Anger followed the thought. Just because he had lain awake remembering how good she had felt in his arms, and how aroused he had been by her kiss didn't mean she felt the same way. She could be calling on perfectly legitimate royal business. At least he had no worries about Amanda this time. His daughter was safely in her room with Mary Jo.

In any event, no matter how much he had enjoyed the experience or how much he craved a repeat, kissing Giselle had been the height of folly. He wasn't about to indulge any more fantasies that could undermine his plans.

He had to think of Amanda. She might be settling

down at Merrisand finally, and had evidently made a friend in Mary Jo, but this wasn't their home. Until he could buy land of his own and make a real home for his daughter, he couldn't afford to let himself get sidetracked.

Giselle could easily become more than a diversion, he knew, and that scared him. Apart from the logic that said a princess wouldn't want a man with so little to offer her, he wasn't about to trust his heart again. After the years of despair trying to save Yvette, he was finished with love for good.

That it might not be finished with him was a terrifying thought.

Unable to see into the passenger compartment through the heavily tinted windows, he approached the car. The driver was Kevin Jordan, the R.P.D. man who had brought Amanda home after she ran away.

"Afternoon, Kevin. Is there something I can do for you?"

The driver got out and lounged against the side of the car. "I'm waiting for the princess. She decided to take a walk in the woods."

Concern lifted the fine hairs on the back of Bryce's neck. "Alone?"

"Not my choice, believe me. But I can't very well throw her over my shoulder and cart her back to the castle." His tone suggested he would have liked to.

Bryce knew how the man felt. "Which way did she go?"

Kevin pushed his thick hair back. "By now she'll be a good way along the path between the castle and the deer park. If I were you, I wouldn't intrude. Her Highness didn't sound as if she'd welcome company."

Welcome or not, she was a princess and Bryce wasn't about to let her wander around the park unescorted, even though the staff were all security screened as was Bryce himself. They were used to being around royalty and knew when to leave well enough alone. But the park was bounded by vast tracts of forest. Impossible to police every inch of it.

Why was he so concerned about her? She knew the hazards probably better than he did. If she chose to wander off alone, why was it any of his business?

He could be breaking all kinds of protocol by going after her but he didn't care. Kissing her was probably the biggest breach of the lot, and he'd done that, hadn't he? She hadn't exactly pushed him away.

Thinking of the hungry way she had kissed him back made his blood heat. She had practically seduced him. Then she had also coolly and calmly suggested they forget the whole thing, he reminded himself as his strides lengthened. If wishes were horses…he thought.

He saw her before she saw him.

He told himself he was glad she wore a man-tailored shirt and pants instead of the ridiculously short linen skirt that had so excited him in her office. But even the severe cut of the clothes couldn't disguise her sensational figure.

His chest tightened. Her hair was loose today, held off her face by a pair of seashell combs set with gold flecks that reflected the sunlight. She looked as if she had stars in her hair. The slight breeze lifted the strands and she kept smoothing them down with her hand. If he buried his face in her hair, would it smell of the breeze? The urge to find out made him want to forget his resolution.

She looked distracted. Sad, he thought, his gut clenching. What—or who—had put that unhappy expression on her lovely face? He reminded himself it wasn't his job to take it away. He approached her anyway. "Lovely afternoon for a walk, Your Highness."

His carefully neutral tone, a far cry from how he felt, had the desired effect. Before his eyes she turned back into a princess, cool and self-assured. She nodded. "Far too beautiful to be shut away indoors."

He couldn't agree more, and he didn't mean the weather. "Can I help you with anything?"

"I came out for some air after being in meetings most of the day. Don't let me intrude on your work."

Go away and let me be miserable in peace, he translated. Not until he knew why she looked so unhappy, and if there was anything he could do to help. So much for resolutions.

"You're not intruding," he assured her. "Apart from some paperwork I can attend to this evening, I'm free to give you the deluxe tour if you like."

"Another time, perhaps. I'm not up to absorbing anything more right now." She walked on and he fell into step beside her.

"Must have been quite a meeting."

The disquiet in his tone made her turn to him. "Robert Gaudet flew back from America to see me today."

"To try to change your mind about him?"

Her eyebrows lifted. "How did you guess?"

"Someone put that doom-laden look on your face."

She gave him a wry smile. "That bad, huh?"

"Bad enough to make me want to hide any handy rope."

This time her smile held genuine amusement. "There's no need. I'm more annoyed that he wouldn't take no for an answer."

Bryce knew how Gaudet felt. If the princess had been his, he wouldn't have given up without a fight, either. But she wasn't, nor did he want her to be. By providing a shoulder to cry on, he was only being a good royal lackey. "I can't say I blame him," he said.

Her steps faltered. "Do you think I'm making a mistake?"

Not a chance, he thought, but said, "Only you can answer that, Your Highness."

"It was Giselle last time we spoke."

Last time they spoke, a lot of things had been different. "I overstepped the mark. It won't happen again." He couldn't afford to let it.

Giselle knew she should appreciate his restraint, but she felt frustrated. She blamed her reaction on Robert's visit, but suspected it wasn't the whole reason. "I haven't seen any of the movie people around the park," she commented.

He frowned. "After I laid down the law about where they could go and what they could do, they left in a huff," he said. "The producer said he was going to take this up with Gaudet. I suspect they'll find another location."

She felt cheered although she shouldn't be. *She* had allowed Robert's people to film in the park. Needing a change of subject, she asked, "How's Amanda?"

"Much happier, thanks to you. Through your sketching group, she's made friends with another newcomer to the school."

"Mary Jo Downey, the American girl?" She had seen the two children giggling together at the castle school.

He nodded. "They're at home now, working on an assignment I believe you gave them."

"Researching ways the Merrisand Trust helps children," she recalled.

"Did you know they visited the Youth Vocational Center to get the story for themselves?"

She smiled with pleasure. "Resourceful of them. The facility is a very worthwhile endeavor."

"So my daughter says. She's decided when she grows up, she's going to be a counselor like her mother."

They had almost reached the lodge, where she could see Kevin Jordan waiting patiently beside her car. Her slowing steps reflected her reluctance to return to the castle just yet. "She must miss her mother very much."

A shadow darkened his features. "We both do. It's not easy for a man to raise a daughter alone. I appreciate the interest you're taking in her."

"There's a wonderful person under her difficult facade. Unfortunately, she's at the age when she doesn't know whether she's a child or a young woman."

"A mother could help her through that."

She brushed his arm with her hand, resisting the urge to leave it there. "You're doing fine. I may not be a mother, but I'm glad to help."

How the devil was he supposed to resist a woman who kissed the way she did, and was as involved with his daughter as he was? "When your car pulled up I was about to take a coffee break. Would you like to join me?" he asked, then cursed himself. What had happened to keeping his distance? "Of course, you probably have a million royal duties."

"Nothing that can't wait," she said, her tone lifting.

He had guessed right, she hadn't wanted to leave yet. "Your driver might like coffee, too," he suggested. He felt guilty for keeping the man hanging around, but definitely didn't want to share Giselle with him.

"I'm sure he'd prefer not to wait. I'll ask him to return for me in an hour."

A few minutes later, the car driving off sounded like a reprieve, although she couldn't say from what. She would have liked to tell Kevin not to come back for a week, but that was impossible. She had already neglected her duties for too long. Another hour would put her even further behind schedule. The awareness didn't stop her heart lightening as she followed Bryce into the lodge.

She was pleased to see that the packing boxes were gone. Pictures hung on the walls and the place had a general air of hominess. No wonder Amanda was settling in at last.

"I'll just check on Amanda and have Mrs. Gray bring us coffee and something to eat," he said, showing Giselle into the living room.

She *was* hungry, she discovered. After the confrontation with Robert, she'd barely touched the working lunch Max had arranged, feeling too churned up to eat. She could imagine what her brother would say if he knew she'd sought refuge in the controller's lodge, but she didn't care. What was the use of being a princess if she couldn't please herself now and again? She didn't do it often.

The thought helped her to relax on the comfortable sofa. Some of the furniture she recognized as antiques belonging to the lodge, but Bryce had added a few pieces of his own, like this tapestry-covered sofa and matching chairs. Their quality reminded her that he had been a man of considerable means before he allowed his grandfather to sell off his previous home.

Why had he agreed? He put a good face on it, but neither he nor Amanda were truly happy at Merrisand. From her research she knew his grandfather was the person behind the sale of Eden Valley, but surely Bryce's parents would have voted in his favor?

Unless he hadn't wanted them to. The place may have reminded him so painfully of his wife that he couldn't bear to stay.

She heard a telephone ring, the sound quickly cut off as the call was answered. She stretched luxuriously. When she left the castle she had neglected to pick up her cell phone, so she wasn't expecting any calls. Other than her bodyguard, no one knew precisely where she was. What a luxury.

She was startled when the door flew open and Bryce stormed in, his expression set. "Elaine Godwin just called," he said.

"How did she track me down?"

"She took a good guess where you'd be," he said shortly. He sounded angry. "She suggests we turn on the TV. She's going to do the same. Evidently the network has been promoting a story she thinks you ought to see. She'll be at your office if you need to contact her after you've seen the show."

Giselle's stomach churned but she resumed her seat. She might have known she would pay for stealing this time to herself. "Is something wrong?"

"You'd better see for yourself."

He strode to a cabinet and flung open a pair of carved doors to reveal a large-screen television set. When he operated a remote control, the screen sprang to life on an afternoon program she rarely watched. Supposedly reporting current affairs, it more often dealt in gossip and scandal, but was one of the most popular in Carramer.

Now she was unsettled to see her own face looming large behind the presenter. She sat forward. What was going on?

"In today's main story, we bring you the news that the romance between Her Highness, Princess Giselle of Taures, and Oscar-nominated actor Robert Gaudet is over."

Footage of herself and Robert filled the screen, then faded back to the presenter. "As you'll hear in our exclusive interview with Robert Gaudet, the wedding bells everyone expected between Carramer's sweethearts won't be happening, thanks to this man."

Giselle gasped as the camera focused on her sketch of Bryce. Shown in close-up, there was no mistaking the loving care she had poured into the drawing.

"This is the man Robert Gaudet says came between the princess and the actor. It was drawn by the princess herself, during a class that included the man's ten-year-old daughter. He is widower Bryce Laws, recently appointed controller of the Royal Deer Park at Merrisand. According to Mr. Gaudet, the sketching class was invented to provide a cover so the couple could meet in secret at the castle."

"That's a lie," Giselle objected out loud. When Robert called from America she had told him about starting the class, never suspecting he would reach such a wildly inaccurate conclusion.

"Truth doesn't seem to concern these people," Bryce observed. His expression was carved in stone, although she noticed that his fingers around the remote were white. "How the devil did they get hold of that drawing?"

She cast her gaze down. "Robert must have taken it from my desk while he waited for me in my office this morning."

"He didn't waste time getting his revenge."

She nodded. "His contacts at the studio would have been only too happy to have the exclusive story of our breakup. They must have rushed it to air as fast as they could."

Bryce frowned. "His version of the story."

"This morning he intimated that our relationship had helped him to obtain backing for his new film project," she said.

"So he couldn't afford to have you drop him publicly."

"He got in first." She twisted her hands together. "It isn't the first time I've been subject to gossip, but I'm sorry you had to be implicated."

He shot her a savage look. "I can handle a few slings and arrows. It's Amanda I'm worried about. How is she going to feel when this is all over the school tomorrow?"

"Oh, Bryce, I'm so sorry."

"Sorry doesn't cut it, Princess," he snapped. "For her sake, there should be an immediate announcement from the castle that this story is a lie concocted by a jilted lover."

Bitterness flooded through her. "You think anyone would believe such a denial?"

He thumbed the remote and the sound became a murmur, then he came to stand over her. "I don't care what they believe. My daughter doesn't deserve this."

Tears stung the backs of her eyes but she blinked them away. She was not going to let him reduce her to tears. "And you think I do?"

His anger faltered, but he said grimly, "As a princess, you must be used to the attention."

"It doesn't mean I enjoy it."

He saw then what she had been struggling to hide from him. Outwardly her royal mask was firmly in place, her back ramrod straight and her expression impassive. It wasn't until he looked into her eyes that he understood the depth of her distress.

Kneeling on the couch beside her with one foot braced on the floor, he grasped her hands. They felt icy. He chafed them between his own to warm them, but only succeeded in warming himself. The report that he had come between her and Gaudet was a lie, he assured himself. It had to be.

But there was the drawing the princess had made of him. He couldn't deny what he had seen for himself, what millions of other people must have seen: the tenderness that spoke from every line. He might be able to convince himself that he felt nothing for her, but what did she feel?

It didn't matter. He crushed the thought. He wasn't about to become involved with her more than he had done already, and that was more than he had intended. "No one enjoys being the focus of gossip and slander," he said.

She dragged in a steadying breath. With her hands

in his, she could feel his pulse racing under her fingers. "I never dreamed Robert felt so strongly about our relationship."

"More like his own career."

She was furiously angry with Robert, but fairness made her say, "His is a tough business."

He pulled his hands free and stood up. "You're making excuses for him. Does that mean you still love him?"

The admission was out before she could prevent it. "I never loved Robert. He was good company, and the first man I've known not to be intimidated by my position." Not the last, she thought but didn't add. Bryce didn't find her intimidating, but theirs was a working relationship, quite different from hers and Robert's. Wasn't it?

Bryce went to a sideboard and poured water from a carafe into two glasses, then brought one to her. "I'll send Amanda away for a few days until this whole thing blows over. Her grandparents didn't want me bringing her to Merrisand. I've been getting e-mails from them almost daily asking when she can come back to visit. They'd be delighted to have her for as long as necessary."

Giselle sipped the water. "She told me you don't approve of them spoiling her."

"That's one of the reasons I took her away from Nuee. Babette and Lyle were trying to turn her into a substitute for the daughter they'd lost. I couldn't blame them, but I couldn't let it continue either. I think they've gotten the message by now, so a few days shouldn't do much harm."

She put the glass down on a side table. "You seem sure this will blow over in a few days."

He cupped his hands around his glass, looking as if he wished it held something stronger than water. "Why wouldn't it?"

"Robert isn't going to let it. He can't afford to. As long as he looks like the injured party, his image is intact and his project stays alive. In some ways, I can't blame him."

Bryce nodded his understanding. "I'd be more charitable if my daughter wasn't caught in the middle." His expression softened fractionally. "It isn't exactly a hardship, having my name romantically linked with a princess."

As long as there was nothing to the rumor, she understood. What else did she expect? A declaration that he was secretly in love with her? She didn't want one, did she? She hadn't finished with Robert to become involved with another man, especially one who was plainly not interested.

"By royal custom, we don't comment on stories about ourselves. If we remain silent, the fuss should subside," she said.

He glanced at the set. In muted tones the presenter was talking about what she termed "the princess's mystery man." Himself, in other words. They had film footage of Eden Valley, some file shots of children from the castle school on an excursion. Thankfully, Amanda wasn't among them. And lots of images of Giselle. How did she stand having her life dissected in public like this?

When they showed pictures of her recent romance with Gaudet, Bryce's mood inexplicably blackened. His heart felt on the verge of seizing, although he refused to think jealousy could be the cause.

He should be focusing on what they were going to do about the situation.

Before he could say anything, the door opened and Amanda stood there. She was breathing fast, and twin spots of color vibrated on her cheeks. "Mary Jo and me had the TV on in my room. They're talking about you, Dad."

The breath left his body in a rush and he looked at the princess. The picture of composure, she had her hands in her lap, her posture more upright than ever. "We have a guest, Amanda," he said quietly.

The child's gaze flew from the television set still playing the story of their supposed romance, to the princess. She bobbed a curtsy. "Sorry, Your Highness. I guess you heard?" When Giselle nodded, Amanda added, "Isn't it amazing?"

He masked his astonishment. "You mean you're not upset, chicken?"

Amanda scuffed her feet, then brightened. "It's kind of cool, seeing you on TV, Dad. They make you sound like a celebrity, like the people in my magazine."

"Except that I'm not a celebrity," he pointed out.

"No, you're only my dad. I mean, you're important, but you're not...well, they made you sound like a pop star or something."

He tried not to wince too obviously as he placed a hand on her shoulder. "You understand that not everything you see on television is true, don't you? We've talked about that often enough."

Amanda rubbed her cheek against his hand. "I know, but I was kind of hoping this would be."

"Would you mind if it were true, Amanda?" Giselle asked.

The child's eyes widened as she absorbed what the princess seemed to be implying. ''You mean you and my dad…you really are…oh, wow.''

Bryce felt slightly stunned himself. ''I take it that's a good wow?''

He reeled as his daughter threw herself at him and planted a kiss on his cheek. ''It's a good wow,'' she agreed. She gave Giselle a shy smile, as if she could hardly believe her ears. ''Oh, wow,'' she said again. ''I have to go tell Mary Jo.''

Before Bryce could say any more, Amanda danced out in a flurry of childish laughter. When he was sure she was no longer within earshot, he whirled on the princess, not caring if he was breaking every rule in the book by raising his voice to her. ''What the devil do you think you're doing?''

Chapter Nine

Giselle wasn't sure herself. She had seen something in Amanda's eyes that tugged at her, making her want to keep the child secure. And loved. That it might be her own need for love she saw reflected there, she also considered.

Bryce hovered over her like an avenging angel. Her heart pounded. The cliché about a man being magnificent when he was angry hardly began to describe him. Although he looked as if he would like to hit her, she felt completely safe. Well, not completely. Safe from harm, anyway. With Bryce, there would always be an element of danger, she suspected.

"She seemed to like the idea of us as a couple," she said, striving to sound calmer than she felt.

He didn't even try. "And that makes it all right to get her hopes sky-high, knowing they have to be dashed when the truth comes out?"

A plan had begun to shape itself in her mind. "Do they have to be dashed?"

She had stopped him, she saw, as a range of emotions from anger to outright disbelief chased across his handsome features. "Are you serious?"

She hadn't known how much until the words left her mouth. Now they made perfect sense. "Why shouldn't we let the world think we're a couple? It would be simpler than trying to deny everything."

He picked up his water glass, looked at it then put it down with an expression of distaste. "You'd go that far to protect Gaudet?"

She hadn't considered such a thing. "Robert has nothing to do with this."

Her hurt tone seemed to defuse some of his anger. "Then what does, Your Highness?"

His use of her title was meant to emphasize the gulf between them. Right now she felt as if it didn't exist. Excitement built inside her, only years of royal training allowing her to remain outwardly composed. "As long as I stay unattached, I'm an easy target for the media. You're only the latest man I'm supposed to be involved with."

His lip curled. "That's comforting."

"I didn't say it's true. If I so much as talk to an available man, I can be sure our supposed romance will be headline news the next day."

"How is going along with the latest rumor supposed to help?"

She laced her fingers together and studied them intently, steadying her breathing so she wouldn't sound emotional when she said, "I had rather more than that in mind."

"You're suggesting we pretend there's a real romance between us?"

He didn't sound bothered by the thought, she noticed. If she hadn't known better, she would have mistaken the huskiness in his voice for interest. It cost her a lot to say, "You don't want a real romance anymore than I do. But I want the media to stop hounding me about my love life. And you want a mother for Amanda."

He held up a hand. "Whoa, Princess. This sounds a lot like a marriage proposal."

Over the pounding of her heart, she asked, "Would you mind if it were?"

"I'd rather be the one making it. If I thought it was a good idea," he added.

"Do you have a better one?"

"Why not tell the truth? That Gaudet concocted the story about you and me to save his own skin."

"We'd only get in deeper," she argued. "Why do you think the royal family never comments on stories about us in the media?"

"What you're suggesting is more than a comment. It's an admission." She remained silent, letting him read what he would into it. After a long pause, he said, "You know I want you, Princess."

In a voice barely above a whisper, she said, "I know." After the heady experience of his kiss, how could she not know?

"I couldn't guarantee to stop at a marriage of convenience."

Tremors rippled through her. "I know that, too."

"You'd accept that, although I'm not willing to love again?"

She heard the pain of experience in his voice. "Neither of us is talking about love. Not romantic love, anyway." All too briefly in his arms, she had tasted the other kind, and her whole being vibrated with the need for more. Why shouldn't they enjoy each other without romantic entanglements?

She thought of her parents who had been brought together by their families and had married because it was expected of them. They were happy enough in their way, weren't they? "Royal marriages have been made for reasons other than love for centuries," she told him.

He could hardly believe he was discussing marriage to the princess so dispassionately. It must be true that royalty did things differently. He couldn't deny that Giselle made his heart beat faster. If he closed his eyes he could feel her lithe body against him, taste the sweetness of her mouth cleaving to his. It wasn't as if he needed her, he told himself, as an aching sensation gripped him. But he did want her.

His daughter needed Giselle, too, in her own way. Since she'd joined the princess's drawing class, he could see the difference the extra attention was making already. In the group, Amanda had not only found her first friend at Merrisand, she'd found a friend in the princess, too. Under Giselle's care, he'd watched Amanda's surliness ebb away.

For the last few months Amanda had been telling him in countless small ways that it was all right with her if he wanted to marry again. She understood he would never forget her mother and that Yvette would always have a place in his heart, but life was for living. If Amanda knew that at ten years old, how could he deny the truth of it at his age?

"Won't your family disapprove?" he asked, feeling his resistance lessen and knowing it wasn't entirely due to logic.

She gave a barely perceptible shrug. "I'm old

enough to make my own choices. In any case, I'm known as the black-sheep princess now, so I may as well give them another reason to disapprove of me.''

''They would have been happier if you'd married Gaudet?''

She nodded. ''In fairness, my family wants me to be happy. But they also want the people to approve of what I do.''

''Will they approve of me?''

It was tempting to sound cynical, but she found she couldn't, not about this. ''Provided we convince them that you swept me off my feet. Love has a way of softening the most hardened critics.''

''I haven't swept you off your feet yet,'' he pointed out.

Yet. The promise implicit in the word sent sensation shimmering through her. He had no idea how close he had come when he kissed her. In all the months they'd been seeing one another, Robert had never made her heart flutter as easily as Bryce had managed to do with a single kiss.

For something to do with her hands, she picked up the water glass and drained it, shaking her head at his gestured offer of a refill. She didn't want water. She rarely drank anything stronger than champagne, but she wished her glass held something more potent now. Something to subdue her inner turmoil.

She wanted to be the one making the running, deciding on the terms. She was afraid that Bryce had already taken the reins out of her hands. ''I think you misunderstand my proposal. I was suggesting an alliance, not a true marriage.''

''Because you want to become Keeper of the Castle,'' he said, his voice hardening. ''Do you think I've forgotten?''

She had managed to. Although she had wanted the position for as long as she could remember, she hadn't given it a thought when she'd suggested marriage to Bryce. She almost laughed out loud. How had he managed to drive such a thought out of her mind?

The same way he drove every other thought away, she concluded. Around him she became befuddled with needs and desires that got in the way of logical thinking. If she'd returned to the castle instead of coming to his home, she might have dealt with the situation more objectively. Her solution, conceived under his influence, was only going to make her life more complicated.

Since she couldn't tell him what she was thinking without revealing the extent of his effect on her, she gave a dismissive laugh, although it didn't quite come off. ''You're right, of course. I do want the job.''

His eyes darkened. ''How much?''

It was her turn to frown. ''I don't understand?''

''Enough to deed the deer park to me?''

She stared at him. ''As a wedding present?''

''You can make it look that way if you wish. I'm prepared to pay the full value of the land, but I'll need some time.''

Icy fingers played along her spine. She hadn't wanted love, but she hadn't expected this. ''You want to bargain with me for my hand in marriage?''

''You said yourself this would be an alliance rather than a real marriage. Both of us should get something out of it.'' He began to tick off points on his fingers. ''Once married, you qualify for the Keeper's job. I gain the mother my daughter badly needs, but one who doesn't expect anything from me that I'm not prepared to give."

Plainly her heart was the only one at risk here. What did she expect? A declaration of undying love? She didn't want that any more than he did, she assured herself. If she did entrust him with her heart, he would be able to control her in ways she didn't want to be controlled. A businesslike arrangement would make sure that didn't happen. So why didn't she feel happier about it?

She shifted restlessly. "I still don't see where the deeds to the park come in."

He folded his arms over his broad chest. "You must know I had my own land before coming to Merrisand?" When she gave a cautious nod, he went on, "I intend to have it again."

"And my part of the deal is to ensure you get what you want."

"As long as you benefit from the arrangement, it's a fair bargain."

Fair perhaps, but difficult to accept, given that Bryce's offer resonated uncomfortably with Robert Gaudet's approach to their relationship. Was she fated to be courted only for what she could give a man? No, she decided, Bryce was different. He may not want love, but he was determined that she would be happy with whatever arrangement they agreed to. Robert had only ever considered his own needs.

"The land is mine to give you," she said slowly. "It is part of my inheritance as Princess of Taures Province. Not the forest beyond. That's part of the national estate. But I can do with the park itself as I choose. We would need a marriage contract, of course."

"Otherwise I could wait until the land was legally mine, then walk away from our marriage." He took a deep breath. "Although I wouldn't."

If she knew nothing else about him, she understood that he would keep his word to his last breath. "No, you wouldn't."

"I'm glad we understand each other. That leaves only one thing."

Before she could ask what it was, he went down on one knee beside her and grasped her hands. His gaze burned into hers with a message impossible to misinterpret. He might not be offering her his heart, but he would be a real husband to her in every other way. "Giselle de Marigny, will you marry me?" he asked.

A shudder shook her. What had she done? Her thoughts flashed back to when she was fourteen and had insisted on riding a horse beyond her experience. He had thrown her, of course, but she had remounted time after time, convinced that the stallion would eventually bow to her will. He never had, and she had learned a bitter lesson. Some things were beyond even her iron willpower. Was marriage to Bryce going to be another such experience?

More memories surfaced. Through stubborn persistence, she had made a friend of the stallion, who had allowed her liberties he permitted no one else. Gradually she had learned that conquering him would have been far less satisfying than meeting him on equal terms, in a relationship forged through mutual respect.

She relaxed her hands in Bryce's. "Yes, I will marry you."

Still keeping hold of her hands, he stood up, his gaze never leaving her face as she moved with him.

When she would have leaned into his embrace, his arms became steel, forcing her to wait, to savor the moment.

"Are you sure?" he asked, his tone a honeyed baritone.

In his arms, she wasn't sure of anything anymore. "I think so."

"You'll need more assurance than that to get through this," he cautioned. "You know how ruthless the media will be?"

She breathed deeply, forcing her heartbeat to slow. "To you, too. You'll have to earn your place in the people's affection."

"As long as I have a place in yours, I'll manage."

"You'll have that, I promise." He didn't love her, but she felt sure that he would be good to her. Perhaps too good. Held no more than a hand span away from him, she ached to be pulled against him and feel his lips commanding hers, a foretaste of the potency of his possession.

Impossible as it seemed, there would be more. They would share a life beyond the bedroom. She could look forward to coming home to him at the end of the day and waking up beside him in the morning. She had never imagined doing that with anyone before. She was surprised how attractive she found the prospect.

He kept his eyes open as he gently covered her mouth with his, seeking, tasting, his tongue tangling with hers until the room started to spin. She clung to him, answering his kiss out of needs she had only acknowledged in the deepest recesses of her soul until now.

She had been shouldering royal responsibilities

since she was old enough to recite her long list of
titles. For one sweet moment, she felt her burdens fall
away, letting her simply be a woman in the arms of
a powerfully desirable man.

Her laughter rippled against his mouth. Around
Bryce nothing was simple. But he was powerfully desirable. Joy bubbled through her, along with an apprehension she couldn't quite subdue. Wanting him
as much as she did, could she really keep her heart
out of the bargain? She was afraid she was going to
find out.

Chapter Ten

Prince Maxim seemed oblivious to the flurry of activity in the gallery as the castle's curatorial staff busied themselves preparing the forthcoming Voyager Exhibition commemorating the first European explorers to visit Carramer. The exhibition wasn't due to open for another couple of weeks, and Giselle and Max were inspecting progress.

She had chosen the neutral location to discuss her plans with him, hoping to avoid a repeat of the scene when she had told her parents about Bryce. Faint hope, she thought, seeing Max's face.

He looked as angry as Giselle had ever seen him, as he said, "I can't believe you want to marry a castle employee."

She had known this wouldn't be easy, having already had to defend her decision to her parents in one of the most tumultuous meetings she had ever had with them. Bryce had wanted to accompany her, but she had been afraid his presence would only make things more difficult. He could formally ask her parents for her hand in marriage after she had paved the way, she told him. For the moment it was better if she went to Taures city alone.

Once her parents realized they weren't going to change her mind, they had reluctantly given the couple their blessing. As Maxim would in time. "Bryce won't be an employee for much longer. I'm deeding the deer park to him as my wedding gift," she said.

Max halted beside a display of fifteenth-century maps by the Portuguese explorer Pedro Fernandez de Quirós. "The park is yours to give, but it seems an unusually generous gift."

Not so generous, given that Bryce had insisted on purchasing the land over time, she thought.

"Has he bewitched you in some way?" Max asked.

She touched a hand to the glass case sheltering the hand-colored maps. "No more than the usual." .

"Are you pregnant?"

Her parents had asked the same question. She hadn't let it throw her then and she wouldn't now, although the fast beating of her heart made her wonder what she would have liked her answer to be. "No, I'm not. I should be offended that you feel the need to ask."

Max's expression softened a little. "I withdraw the question. But these are the questions that the people will ask when your engagement is announced. You must agree this is sudden? For weeks, we've all been anticipating the wedding of the year between the princess and the star. Suddenly the star is gone, replaced by an unknown rancher."

Idly, Giselle traced on the glass the familiar outline

of Carramer, drawn by a man from half a world away who had risked everything to venture into the unknown. By marrying Bryce, wasn't she doing something similar? "Bryce is more than a rancher. He has substantial holdings in his family company both here and in the United States."

Max nodded tautly. "I know. I had the R.P.D. check him out soon after we met, before he took over the deer park. He may not be royal, but his pedigree is impressive. You do know he fell out with his family after his wife died? That's why his land was auctioned."

"He fell out with his grandfather because he wouldn't follow orders."

"Yet you expect such a man to follow royal dictates? Ours isn't an easy life. Commoners don't always take to it as readily as they expect."

"If the monarch of Carramer and his brother can marry commoners and be blissfully happy, why can't the princess of Taures Province?"

When Max didn't respond, Giselle looked around. The head curator, Leah Landon, was directing the placement of a fall-front bureau believed to have been used by English explorer Captain James Cook during his voyages around the South Pacific in the 1600s.

Absent from the scene was Leah's right-hand woman, Kirsten Bond. Kirsten had recently become engaged to Giselle's cousin, Rowe Sevrin, Viscount Aragon. "You didn't find it a problem when Rowe fell in love with Kirsten," Giselle reminded her brother.

Max followed her gaze. "Rowe has never been what you'd call a model member of the royal family."

"And I have?"

He was forced to smile. "Perhaps not. Maybe I'm so resistant to the idea of you marrying Bryce Laws because I don't have the luxury of choosing whom I marry."

Under an ancient agreement, the prince of Taures was required to marry a woman of royal birth, regardless of his personal feelings. She had always thought the restriction unfair and was glad that she had far more freedom.

"It's probably just as well to have new blood in the family," Max added.

It took Giselle a heartbeat to realize that he was giving in. "You are happy for me, aren't you?" she asked, hoping she was reading him correctly.

"I'd be happier if I thought you were marrying for love."

She lifted her head. "What other reason would I have?"

He gestured around them. "I know how badly you want to become Keeper of the Castle."

"And you think that's why I'm marrying Bryce? If that's all I wanted, I could marry Robert and make everybody happy."

Max's gaze narrowed. "Why aren't you?"

"I don't love Robert." She was afraid he would take over control of her life from Max, she thought but didn't say, knowing her brother wouldn't appreciate the comparison.

She didn't for one minute believe that Bryce was more manageable. The opposite, she thought, suppressing a shiver. He was more of a man than Robert Gaudet would ever be. But Bryce had his own reasons for wanting to marry her and they didn't include exerting mastery over her. At least she didn't think they did. As long as they both gained from the alliance, it would work, she decided, hoping she wasn't deluding herself.

The prince paused in front of a display of botanical specimens gathered by the French explorer, La Pérouse. Among them she recognized some rare Carramer orchids.

Max studied the pressed flowers with their handwritten descriptions in flowing French copperplate for a few minutes before turning to her. "I have one request to make."

She managed a smile. "Only one?"

He gestured impatiently. "This is serious, Giselle. As your prince and older brother, I ask that you delay announcing your engagement to Laws until you've had a chance to get to know him better."

Max didn't know it, but their parents had made a similar request. She was still trying to decide how to respond. "What should I do about the speculation in the media?"

His shoulders lifted expressively. "Let them speculate. It won't be the first time."

Max probably expected her to tire of Bryce as she had apparently tired of Robert, but it wasn't going to happen. Still, the request wasn't unreasonable. "Very well, we'll say nothing for the moment. But I won't sneak around pretending nothing's going on between us."

"I don't expect you to. If you're seen together, it will help prepare the way for when you make your engagement public."

"Soften the blow, you mean?"

Her brother smiled. "Robert Gaudet was a popular choice for you."

"Do you think I should marry to satisfy popular choice?"

He covered her hand with his. "I think you should follow your heart."

Following her heart wasn't as simple as her brother made it sound, she soon learned. Bryce had agreed to Max's request to delay announcing their engagement until they knew one another better, and had suggested a series of dates at locations where castle security was able to shadow them.

Even so, the media had pursued them like hounds on a scent trail. In spite of the diligence of the security people, a drive through the Great Park, dinner at a secluded restaurant, even a quiet evening spent at the royal residence within the castle, were all reported and photographed in disturbing detail.

To shield Amanda from the fanfare, Bryce had arranged for her and her friend, Mary Jo, to spend the school holiday with Amanda's maternal grandparents on Nuee. Giselle had provided a plane from the royal fleet and sent her equerry to escort the girls. Starry-eyed with excitement about her new status as the daughter of the princess's romantic interest, Amanda had been reluctant to go but had accepted Bryce's assurance that it was only for the vacation.

From their phone calls, the princess gathered that both girls were having a wonderful time. The grandparents lived near the beach and had arranged for the girls to have windsurfing lessons.

So far the media had been too preoccupied with Bryce and Giselle to focus on Amanda, but Giselle feared the respite wouldn't last. She was used to having her life dissected in the popular press, but she could see Bryce becoming more and more annoyed. If the spotlight switched to Amanda, he was likely to go crazy.

"What did you expect? You are marrying a princess," she said when he showed her yet another paper carrying a picture of them taken covertly with a telephoto lens. The photo showed her wearing a crocheted bikini and lying on a chaise beside the outdoor pool. Wearing navy swim shorts, Bryce sat on the edge of the pool beside her. They had only been talking, but the photo made it look far more intimate than that.

Imagining the photographer lining them up in his sights from up a ladder outside the castle wall, she shuddered and glanced uneasily out the window. Was a telephoto lens trained on them now, as they ate lunch in the morning room at the castle? All she could see was the greenery crowding the window, but that didn't mean a paparazzo wasn't crouched in the bushes. The R.P.D. should have made sure there wasn't, but they hadn't had much success keeping cameras away from them at the pool.

As if reading her thoughts, Bryce looked toward the window. "You sound as if you enjoy the attention."

Masking her hurt, she said, "I'm used to it. That doesn't mean I enjoy it."

His gaze raked the newspaper photo. "If you'd worn a more modest swimsuit, this might not have happened."

Sudden realization washed over her. "You're jealous."

"If by that you mean I care whether the population of Carramer sees my bride-to-be half-naked, perhaps I am."

Indignation overcame her momentary pleasure. Being answerable to Bryce was definitely not part of their agreement. "I was wearing a perfectly decent bikini. Even so, I don't see that it's any concern of yours."

Before she could blink he came around the table and towered over her. "I warned you I wasn't interested in a marriage of convenience."

She struggled for composure, although her heart was double-timing. When she was sure her breathing wouldn't betray her, she said, "You warned me you wouldn't settle for a celibate marriage. It doesn't change the fact that ours will be a marriage of convenience."

A footman bustled in bearing their desserts, frothy concoctions of ripe local cherries layered with meringue. If the man sensed the tension in the room, he didn't acknowledge it, but served them as impassively as if Bryce had been seated opposite the princess at the table, instead of standing over her, his face as black as an approaching storm.

When they were alone again, Bryce reached around her and locked the door. The gesture sent an unwarranted thrill through her. "Perhaps we should rethink this whole idea," he said.

To her amazement, Giselle's mind instantly rejected this. Not because she wanted to marry him, she told herself, but because it was such a perfect solution to many of their problems. When Bryce had gently broached their plans with Amanda, there had been no mistaking the child's enthusiasm. And Giselle had already begun preparing to take over the job of Keeper. Her position would become official as soon as the marriage took place. "You can't," she dismissed.

His eyes blazed. "There's been no official announcement yet."

Giselle toyed with her dessert before pushing it away. "Amanda would be terribly disappointed."

"Better now than later," he said evenly. "I note you didn't say you'd be disappointed."

She twisted her monogrammed napkin into a rope. "Of course I would." More than she wanted to admit to herself.

He planted both arms either side of her, trapping her in the chair. "Because you wouldn't get the job you want so badly?"

It took courage to meet his gaze without flinching. "Naturally."

"For no other reason?"

What did he expect her to say? That the more time they spent together, the more she wanted to marry him for his own sake? The truth of it both alarmed and exhilarated her, although she did her best to subdue the feelings. He didn't want love in his life again, and if he suspected that she was starting to care for him...

No, she wasn't looking for love anymore than he was. She might need a husband to achieve her heart's desire, but her heart was the last organ she would allow to get involved. "What other reason can there be?" she asked.

For a long time, he merely looked at her. Then with infinite care, he grasped her arms and eased her up from the chair until their bodies were aligned. The napkin slid onto the table. ''I can think of at least one.''

He had come to her from the deer park, supposedly to discuss plans to release a new group of sun deer into the forest, and she had given in to impulse and suggested they eat lunch together. Now she dragged in a deep breath, her senses swamped by the scent of the outdoors, and his compelling masculinity that assailed her.

Dressed for work in an open-necked khaki shirt and snug-fitting pants tucked into carved leather boots, he looked heart-stoppingly male. In his grasp, she swayed slightly, overcome by his nearness and her own confused response. Theirs was supposed to be a relationship of convenience, so why did he make her feel so needy?

As if he sensed what she tried to hide from him, he bent his head and feasted on her parted lips, plunging his tongue deep until she couldn't restrain a moan of pure pleasure.

Just a taste, he told himself. A few seconds' respite from the tension imposed on them by being under constant scrutiny. He was strong enough to enjoy her beauty and her passion and keep his emotions out of the equation. Strong enough to keep her emotions safe as well, he told himself.

Exactly how safe his were, he was no longer certain. Seeing that picture on the front page of the newspaper, taken beside the pool, had made him crazier than it had any right to do. He had felt violated for her sake, and his own.

What that signified, he didn't like to think.

So he stopped thinking and drowned himself in her, breathing in the scent of her—something French and expensive and so elusive that it had to be made especially for her. His senses reeled.

He wasn't the only one, he saw when he opened his eyes to feast on her beauty. She had linked her hands around his neck and was clinging to him for dear life. Her lips, parted on a gasp of astonishment that he shared, were too inviting. He plunged again, deeper this time, drawing out the kiss until desire almost overcame logic.

Every nerve in his body screamed to continue, to go deeper still until she was completely his. He hadn't lied about wanting her, but he was beginning to think he had lied about keeping emotion out of it. To himself most of all.

He gently released her, keeping his arms around her to steady her, not because he couldn't bear to let her go. She looked as shaken as he felt.

"What in Merrisand's name was that all about?"

He tried to make his tone light. "A kiss. Something for the next edition of the paper."

Her alarmed gaze darted to the window, and he tightened his hold. "I'm joking. There's no one watching."

Her shiver told him she wasn't amused. "You can't be sure."

"There is one way."

He strode to the window and pressed the button that operated the drapes. They swept closed, plunging the room into haze. He reached for the light but her hand stayed him. "I like it like this."

If they stayed in the gloom, with his internal temperature still sizzling, he wouldn't answer for the consequences. "We have work to do," he said, sounding every bit as apologetic as he felt. Not because the work was being neglected. He hadn't given it a thought since he joined her. But because he couldn't, in good conscience, spend the afternoon the way every instinct drove him to do.

Yesterday the princess had walked him through an exhibition of old maps and charts being set up in one of the public galleries. He had been intrigued by a fifteenth-century map showing the ocean around Carramer as the edge of the world, with the stern warning, "Here be dragons."

In the uncharted waters of his relationship with the princess, here be dragons indeed, he thought. Demons of air and darkness, inviting him to risk the very thing he had promised himself he wouldn't involve: his heart.

Never again.

Never?

He snapped on the light and pulled out her chair for her. She sat with obvious reluctance, plainly puzzled by the abrupt change in his mood. No more than he was himself. He unlocked the door then resumed his seat across the table from her, hating the expanse of cherry wood that separated them, yet needing the buffer. "We need a few rules," he said, hearing his voice come out betrayingly husky.

She laced her fingers together and stared down at them. "Rules set by you, I assume?"

He cleared his throat. "Mutually agreed."

"Just as well. For a moment there, I thought you might turn into Max on me."

Whatever he felt for her, brotherly wasn't even on the list. "I know you don't want me running your life." She had told him so in no uncertain terms.

"Nor do I want anything more than a mother for my daughter."

Liar, liar, a small inner voice chanted. He ignored it. "So we have to find a way to make a marriage work between us without compromising those needs."

"Do you think we compromised them just now?"

He heard the tremor she tried to keep out of her voice. "I darn well know we did." He had been on the verge of a lot more compromising, until sanity set in.

"What do you suggest as an alternative?"

His thoughts raced. "Not so much an alternative as a way to prove to ourselves that we can make this work. A Wedding Eve."

He heard her small indrawn breath, but she smoothed it out and kept her expression calm. Royal training obviously had its uses. "We're not officially engaged yet. How will spending some time together in seclusion help?" she asked.

"Celibate seclusion," he emphasized. It was the last thing he wanted, and the first thing he had to get right if they were to have a marriage they could live with. "You know as well as I do that the custom doesn't require an official engagement. It merely allows a couple to have some time alone together. In our case, it means getting away from reporters and prying cameras. Away from hovering servants and bodyguards."

"The media will report that we're undertaking a Wedding Eve."

"Let them. They can't say much more than they've already done." He gestured toward the newspaper. "And this time we'll make sure we're not followed."

"What do you hope to prove?"

That he could be around her without getting in over his head, he thought. Out loud, he said, "To make sure we're compatible in more ways than the physical."

"A Wedding Eve would certainly give us that chance." With no divorce in Carramer, the tradition of the Wedding Eve had evolved to allow a couple to ensure they knew one another as fully as possible. It didn't always work. Total isolation was more than some couples could handle without falling into bed together. But ideally, he and Giselle could resist temptation.

"I wasn't aware we had to be compatible," she observed.

Damn her royal reserve. Why weren't her feelings in as much turmoil as his? Was he the only one having trouble with the idea of a marriage of convenience? Then he saw that she had retrieved her napkin and was pleating it into dozens of tiny folds. She wasn't as calm as she wanted him to think. For some reason, the discovery excited him. It shouldn't, because he already knew that they turned one another on. What he needed to discover was if they could avoid doing it. If they could be a couple without needing more.

"It's one way to find out if we can live together as man and wife," he pointed out, feeling his heart strum.

Her lambent gaze lifted to his. "It is, isn't it?" She sounded as if it was the first time she had fully considered where this was leading. He heard the shell of her royal reserve crack a little as she asked, "How soon would you like our Wedding Eve to take place?''

He took satisfaction in cracking her shell even more. ''Amanda is away for a few more days. What's wrong with the day after tomorrow?''

Chapter Eleven

He must be crazy. The forty-eight hours Bryce had given himself was barely enough time to get organized so the deer park wouldn't fall apart while he was with Giselle. The assistant controller had served the royal family for three years. With experience, the man would eventually be able to run the whole show, but he wasn't ready yet.

Catching himself in mid-thought, Bryce blanked the computer screen and tilted his chair back. Was he turning into a clone of his grandfather? Now *there* was an alarming thought.

He straightened the chair and picked up the phone. His assistant's astonishment at being given total control, even if it was only for a couple of days, was enough to convince Bryce that he needed to delegate more. He would, he promised himself. No way was he treating anyone else the way his grandfather had treated him.

Although even leopards could change their spots.

He clicked on the e-mail he had received from his grandfather earlier in the day. It seemed that the old man had married again without telling anyone and had turned over control of the family company to Bryce's parents.

Bryce's new grandmother was a nurse who had cared for Karl Laws after the yachting accident that had left him in a wheelchair. Bryce could almost hear his grandfather's dry chuckle as he wrote that she was a child bride, a mere fifty to Karl's seventy-three. She had masterminded their elopement under the pretext of taking Karl to the hospital for tests. They planned to live in Hawaii where his new bride had family, his grandfather wrote.

Bryce's mouth eased into a grin. So Karl had finally met someone who could rule him the way he had ruled Bryce and his family. Pity the old man hadn't remarried before Eden Valley had to be sold.

Not that Bryce was complaining about the way things had worked out. At the old place, someone would always have been looking over his shoulder, his father if not his grandfather. Once he repaid the princess, and that would be as quickly as he could arrange it, he would own this place outright. He would have to build a residence befitting her position, of course. The lodge was roomy and comfortable, but it hardly compared with the castle. He had resigned himself to living at Merrisand after they were married, until their own home was completed.

In his mind, he pictured an imposing house built of local stone and timber, set against the forest surrounds. Saw himself sweeping Giselle into his arms and over the threshold. She'd laugh, and he would kiss her as he carried her up a wide, curving staircase to their suite.

Wrong image, he thought. Theirs was a marriage made with the head, not the heart. He wasn't going to fall in love with her. The reminder didn't stop his deeper needs struggling to surface. Ramming them down with reason didn't help.

He wanted her. How much hardly bore thinking about. He knew she wanted him, but she wanted to be Keeper of the Castle far more. Enough to enter into a cold arrangement to marry a man she didn't love. He found himself shaking his head. However their marriage turned out, it wouldn't be cold. From his fleeting taste of Giselle, he knew she was too fiery, too passionate.

He could console himself that she was wonderful with Amanda, already coaxing her out of her shell until she was almost back to the delightful child he cherished. He could appreciate that the princess had made it possible for him to have his own land in return for helping her to achieve her life's ambition. All true.

What was becoming impossible was convincing himself that she didn't matter to him beyond any of these things.

She would be horrified if she knew. She had chosen him precisely because she didn't want to be fettered by love. She wanted freedom. Paradoxically, because of who she was, she had to marry to get it, but only to a man who demanded nothing of her, certainly not her heart.

Could Bryce marry her and remain uninvolved? The Wedding Eve would let him find out before it was too late.

* * *

He was telling himself he wasn't waiting for her when he heard her helicopter land. His mood had blackened until he almost told her that this wasn't going to work, they were wasting one another's time.

Then he saw her radiant expression and the way the sun haloed her hair and put roses into her cheeks. She looked like a model in camel-colored pants tucked into soft ankle boots, and a buttery silk shirt, the royal version of casual, he supposed. The sun at her back turned the shirt translucent, the effect playing havoc with his vow to remain unaffected. She had such a fine body, slender yet rounded in all the right places. What idiot had decreed that a Wedding Eve should be celibate? he wondered.

He had arranged for them to spend the time in a riverside cottage within the park. He would have liked to whisk her away somewhere more distant, but had drawn the line at taking staff along, so was forced to remain where her security people could guard her from a distance, and where he could be reasonably sure they wouldn't be observed by the media.

Reading his expression, she asked, ''Is something wrong?''

He handed his overnight bag to the bodyguard hovering behind her. ''Nothing's wrong.''

''You look so grim.'' She sounded as uncertain as he felt.

He tried to relax his features. ''Did you have much trouble getting the time away?''

''Getting time to myself is always a challenge. In the end, I simply told Elaine to cancel everything until Monday.''

''How does that feel?''

A smile tilted up the corners of her mouth. "Like I've run away."

The idea of running away with her appealed to him far more than it should. He followed her into the helicopter and the bodyguard jumped in after them, slamming the door shut.

A few minutes later they touched down in a clearing beside the river. It was still early, and the placid water steamed. The bodyguard looked reluctant to leave them alone, but that rather defeated the idea of a Wedding Eve, Bryce thought. They had agreed that the man would fly back to the lodge and wait there in radio contact in case he was needed.

Hopefully he wouldn't be.

As the sound of the helicopter died away, he saw Giselle release a deep breath. "My grandmother spent her Wedding Eve at the Water Pavilion. How did you discover it?"

He walked beside her toward the pavilion. "I was following some wild sun deer by helicopter planning how to introduce some farm-bred stock to the herd, when I spotted the neglected building from the air. I thought it would make an appealing retreat, so I had it cleaned up."

Giselle had last visited the pavilion a year ago and knew how neglected it had been. Now she drew a breath of admiration. Cleared of encroaching greenery, the rough-sawn limestone entrance glowed softly in the morning light.

The pavilion was named for a pebble-lined stream that flowed around the living room and out to a lily pond near the entrance. A glass step crossed the stream and led to the bedrooms, whose glass walls looked out onto a fernery.

"You've done wonders," she said. It was almost as if he had known they would need a private retreat. Her nerves jangled. Marrying Bryce as a business proposition was one thing, but spending a night alone with him in such an idyllic setting was quite another. She tried to imagine being here with Robert and couldn't. With Bryce it was surprisingly easy. She had to throttle off the visions making her knees feel weak.

"I hope you don't mind my cooking," he said when they went inside.

She arched her eyebrows at him. "What's wrong with mine?"

His expression was frankly skeptical. "You can cook?"

"Cordon bleu, Paris," the princess explained.

"If I'd known, I'd have had more exotic provisions sent in."

She wandered into the kitchen, finding a lavish hamper of gourmet foods, as well as a bottle of champagne and chocolate truffles. "This looks fine," she called, then turned to find him right behind her. "This looks fine," she repeated more softly, her throat inexplicably raw.

Her hair fell around her shoulders. He toyed with a strand. "It looks fine to me, too."

She guessed he didn't mean the food, and her pulse jumped. "Shouldn't we explore the rest of the pavilion?"

His eyes became luminous. "There's only the bedrooms."

The last place she dared go with him, feeling as sensitized as she did. "I'm sure they're fine, too," she managed to say. "I'll make us some coffee." Or she would if he would give her some breathing space.

He moved away stiffly, as if his limbs wouldn't quite cooperate. She understood the feeling. "Wouldn't champagne better suit the occasion?" he asked.

Already intoxicated by his nearness, she didn't need alcohol. On the other hand, the idea was to prove that they could handle a marriage of convenience without wanting more. She threw caution to the wind. "Champagne it is."

He poured some into crystal flutes then lifted his glass. "What shall we drink to?"

Survival was the first thing that sprang to her mind. Marrying Bryce was a mad idea. How could she possibly become his wife knowing how much she lov—, um, liked him? She took a gulp of the bubbly liquid, aware that the wrong word had nearly slipped out. Thank goodness she hadn't blurted it out loud, when it was the last thing he wanted from her.

Over the rim of the glass, his gaze also heated. "If you can't think of anything, I propose a toast—to cooking."

She almost choked on champagne. "Cooking?"

"Melding diverse ingredients to create something new," he explained.

That was how he saw their marriage, she interpreted, uncomfortably aware that his toast could also describe the act of procreation. They hadn't even discussed children. She looked forward to being a mother to Amanda, and she also hoped to have children of her own in time. She touched her glass to his, not sure quite what she was drinking to in the end.

When they'd finished, he asked, "Would you like to swim?"

She shook her head. "A walk perhaps."

"It feels strange having nothing to do," she mused. Even stranger being alone with Bryce without the distraction of servants. Should she take his hand as they strolled along the riverside path?

He solved the problem by tucking her hand into the crook of his arm. "You should do this more often."

Her heart flip-flopped. "Share a Wedding Eve?"

"Do nothing."

"It's not so easy in my position."

"Nor in mine," he agreed.

"Surely you can do as you please?"

He exhaled heavily. "I'd almost forgotten how."

She swiveled to look at him. "Because of your wife's illness?"

"Plus my grandfather's demands. He had the controlling interest in the family company that owned our ranch on Nuee. He liked things done his way."

So she'd been right. "You let the place be sold, rather than give in to him?"

As if barely aware of the gesture, he lifted their joined hands, his lips grazing her knuckles, making her whole being shiver. "That was part of it. Amanda was my biggest worry."

Giselle caught her lower lip between her teeth. "What did Amanda have to do with your decision to sell up?"

"I didn't want her to feel pressured to follow me into the family business, the way my grandfather had pressured me. I wanted to show her that she could make her own choice in life, provided she wanted it enough and was willing to do whatever it took. I don't expect you to understand.''

His tenderness pulled the admission from her. ''Oh, but I do. Many times I've wished I could follow my own path.''

His hands slid to her shoulders, kneading away her tension. ''Are you following it now?''

Desire spilled through her, hot and sweet. ''I'm here, aren't I?''

''The question is, why?''

Tension threaded through her. ''This is our Wedding Eve.''

He moved away, resting a hand against the speckled bark of a painted eucalypt that overhung the river. ''But what does it mean to you?''

She struggled against offering the platitudes she sensed he would scorn. ''It means learning whether we can forge a union out of our diverse personalities and needs.''

''And if we can't?''

The gruff question caught her unawares. Was he trying to tell her he had changed his mind? Or that he feared she might? She lifted her head, surprising hope and, yes, apprehension in his dark gaze, although both were quickly masked. Knowing she was playing with fire, but unable to make herself care, she said, ''Kiss me, and you'll have your answer.''

With a sound that was half growl, he pulled her into his arms, the fierceness of his passion making her blood sing. No gentle seduction this. His mouth cleaved to hers, open and demanding, his teeth nipping, his tongue plunging.

Riding waves of sensation, she answered him in kind, hungry for everything he wanted to give her, giving of herself in return as she had never done before.

The air around her felt electrified. She half expected her hair to crackle when he pulled her head back to expose her throat to his kisses. A moan bubbled up, barely recognizable as her own, as she wrenched her head free to fasten her lips to his. She had invited this, wanted it, gloried in it, and she let her greedy mouth tell him so.

His hands were everywhere, exploring, stroking, making her burn with the need for greater closeness. Laboring to catch her breath, she tugged his shirt free, unbuttoned it and skimmed her fingers over the work-forged muscles and taut skin of his chest for the sheer pleasure of it.

Here in the forest depths, beside the ribbon of dark water, she wasn't a princess. She was a wood nymph and he was her satyr. When he bent his head to rain kisses along the cleft between her breasts, she purred with pleasure.

He was why she was here, she thought with what little coherence remained. Not because he could help her attain her ambition, but because he *was* her ambition. How could she have been so blind to the truth of it?

She had agreed to marry him because she loved him. The seed had been sown the night of the masked ball, when he had breached the invisible barrier around her and her defenses as well, although she hadn't known that until now.

How did she begin to number his virtues? If she started counting, would she ever stop? His readiness to give up everything to be his own man and his devotion to his daughter were just two qualities Giselle loved about him.

His kisses were definitely another.

The ground shifted beneath her as he laved her sensitized skin with his tongue. Her whole body sang a siren song of need. In another heartbeat he would pull her down to the mossy bank and she would offer not a shred of resistance. They would become lovers.

Lovers but not in love. The cold truth shocked her into awareness of the life stretching ahead of her. If they made love she would be lost forever, loving him although he had made it clear he didn't welcome her love.

She was forced to accept that sometimes her best efforts weren't enough to change reality. Marrying Bryce knowing he didn't want her love was too high a price to pay, even to become Keeper of the Castle.

Stop this now or you never will, she ordered herself. Still it took almost more strength than she possessed to free herself from his arms. Groping blindly behind her, she felt for the painted eucalypt and gripped the trunk for dear life. Her breathing came in great, heaving gulps. When she felt steadier, she released her death grip and slowly began to tidy her clothes, her shaking fingers making the task a near impossibility.

Bryce watched her with eyes of flame. With his shirt open and his magnificent chest bare, he looked like a warrior king out of Carramer's past, tempting her almost beyond reason to return to his embrace. ''What is it, Giselle? Did I hurt you?'' he asked.

He would if she let him, she thought. Far more than he had already. She crossed her arms over her chest. ''No, but this isn't what a Wedding Eve is all about.''

Some of the flames faded from his gaze. "It's about getting to know one another."

"Beyond the physical," she stated.

He dragged a hand through his hair. "I admit, I got carried away. But I thought—so did you. Was I wrong?"

He must know he wasn't. "It's still a mistake. I can't go through with our wedding."

He looked stunned. "Because I couldn't keep my hands to myself?"

She fiddled with the tree bark. "I didn't want you to, but I've come to my senses. I don't want to marry anyone. It's not personal, Bryce."

He stormed closer. "The hell it isn't. Do you still have feelings for that actor?"

She hadn't given Robert a thought in days. "I already told you I don't," she said. What would Bryce say if she confessed that she loved him? Probably abandon her so fast her head would spin. At least this way, it was her decision. Somehow she mustered her voice. "I'll stand by my agreement to sell you the deer park, and remain as a mentor to Amanda if you'll allow it."

"It's hardly the same as being a mother to her, is it?"

She might have known his main concern would be the effect on his daughter. Not a word about Giselle being a wife to him. What did she expect? A declaration of love she knew he wasn't interested in making?

She spread her hands. "I don't think anything else will work."

His expression was bleak. "And you're obviously not going to try."

"I thought I could, but…"

"You've decided to take the easy way out instead," he finished for her.

"You don't know what you're talking about."

His expression was thunderous. "Then enlighten me. One minute you were melting in my arms, and in the next it's all over. Why the sudden change of heart?"

"Maybe I had to be shown how much of my independence I'd be giving up."

"Was that all the kiss meant to you?"

She nodded dumbly. The kiss had meant far, far more but she couldn't say so without revealing how she really felt. Nor could she stay. The longer they were alone together, the more she risked breaking down and telling him she'd fallen in love with him, when it was the last thing he would want to hear.

As he spun away from her, she caught his arm. "I'm sorry about everything."

She felt his muscles tighten as he said, "Believe me, so am I."

His biting tone shook her, although it was no more than she'd invited. Feeling as she did for him, she had hoped, foolishly it seemed now, that they could remain friends. Her decision was more an act of desperation than he could possibly guess. Not what she wanted at all. And since she couldn't have that…her sigh of regret whispered between them, and she took her hand away. "I'd better leave."

He hesitated, and she wondered if he was going to try to talk her out of going. What would she do then? But the moment passed and he said, "I'll call your pilot. Your helicopter will be here within minutes."

He headed back toward the pavilion. Following

him with dragging steps, she told herself she had done the right thing, the only thing. Better to suffer this short, sharp burst of agony now than endure the never-ending torment of a marriage where all the love was on her side. The assurance didn't provide as much comfort as it should have done.

Chapter Twelve

"**Y**ou're not even looking, Dad."

Bryce dragged his attention back to Amanda, who was waiting for him to comment on a drawing she planned to enter in a school exhibition. Her charcoal sketch of the head of a sun deer was astonishingly lifelike. "It's wonderful, chicken," he said, kissing her on the forehead.

Her eyes brightened. "You really think so?"

"I really think so. At the risk of making you swollen-headed, you're getting frighteningly good."

She took the drawing from him. "That's because of Miss Giselle's sketching class. I'd never have made as much progress without her. I can't wait to see what she thinks of this. Are you dropping me off today?"

He hadn't been near the castle for four days, since the abortive Wedding Eve. He still hadn't found a way to tell Amanda that he and the princess she idolized weren't to be married after all. Coward, he told himself. He would have to tell Amanda soon. The longer he delayed, the more chance there was of her finding out from another source. He wasn't looking forward to telling her.

Since he couldn't stay behind the walls of the deer park forever, he nodded. He would break the news to Amanda after the class, he promised himself.

He hadn't counted on the effect of seeing Giselle again. When he dropped Amanda at the conservatory, the princess was already there. The sight of her made his gut clench with the need to hold her, to have her in his life again. Instead of staying at the back of the group, as he usually did, he told Amanda he would return for her when the class ended. He set out to walk off his pent-up emotions in the castle grounds, aware of Giselle's gaze following him. Beyond a curt greeting, he hadn't been able to bring himself to speak to her.

They had flown back to the lodge in silence, his baffled and angry, hers so pained that it had torn at his heart. He still didn't know what he had done wrong. As far as he could tell, she had simply changed her mind.

Leaving the royal residence, he strode toward Prince's Gate, intending to lose himself in the park outside the castle wall. Instead he found his steps veering toward Parade Hill and the Galleries. Being out in the woods would remind him too much of kissing Giselle by the riverside.

He told himself he didn't care. She was entitled to do as she pleased. He was only angry for Amanda's sake. But part of him recognized the truth. He was hurt and angry for himself, although that made no sense.

Unless he had done the unthinkable.

Slowing, he planted a hand on the castle's ancient stonework to ground himself, heedless of the curious glances from the tourists wandering in the grounds. Possibility seeped into his awareness as surely as the stone's chill percolated his touch. Against all common sense, had he fallen in love with Giselle? Nothing else fully explained the aching emptiness he'd felt since she told him she wouldn't marry him.

Could he have prevented himself falling for her? He had tried, certainly. Believed he had succeeded until her kisses transported him to a heaven he'd believed was forever lost to him. Telling himself the attraction was purely chemical had helped. But only for a time.

There was her gentle sense of humor and her keen interest in the things that interested him. She hadn't had to come and watch him release the new deer into the wild, but she had made the time, as fascinated as he had been with the tentative way the creatures had sniffed the free air, then bounded into the forest with squeaking cries he'd swear were of joy.

Nor was she responsible for his daughter, yet the princess had befriended Amanda and encouraged her interests until the child felt she was a part of castle life. Through the princess's sketching group, his child had made friends and developed a talent that could well bloom into a future career.

His need to be master of his own land hadn't escaped the princess either, and she had found a way to make it possible. Strained as things were between them, she hadn't reneged on her promise. The deeds had arrived on his desk the previous morning, with no mention of financial arrangements. She had simply accepted his word that he would do his part.

He thought furiously. If he had been busy falling for her, what had she been doing? He punched the wall, welcoming the vibration that shivered along his arm, as a further dose of reality. His suspicion grew. Had she been falling in love with him, too?

She knew that he didn't want love, because he had told her. He had even believed it. If she had been falling in love with him, would she have feared his rejection? Enough to want to get in first, before he could hurt her?

When she'd been little, Amanda had scribbled in crayon on a newly painted wall. Told that she couldn't have any ice cream as punishment, she had stubbornly denied ever wanting the promised treat. Only the tears welling in her eyes had told him how disappointed she was. He'd given her the ice cream eventually, and a hug to take away her pain. But not until he'd made her watch him scrub away the mess.

Was Bryce himself the treat that Giselle now denied wanting? The hurt he had seen in her eyes when she moved away from him suggested he was on the right track. He gave vent to a sigh of frustration. Ice cream wasn't likely to take away her pain.

But a hug might. After he'd cleaned up the mess he'd made of courting her.

He levered himself off the wall and spun around. He'd walked long enough for the class to be over soon. He would ask Mary Jo's father to take Amanda home. If Bryce was right, he and the princess had some serious hugging to do.

In a fever of anticipation, he almost cannoned into Prince Maxim, only the other man's evasive action preventing a collision.

"My apologies, Your Highness," Bryce said formally.

A smile hovered on the prince's lips. "Shouldn't you call me Max, since we're to be brothers-in-law?"

So Giselle hadn't told her brother, either. If Bryce had read her feelings aright, maybe they wouldn't have to. "Sounds good to me, Max."

"Walk with me. I'm returning to the executive suites."

A request, not a command, Bryce noted with satisfaction as he fell into step beside the prince. For a time they talked about the deer park, and how impressed the prince was with Bryce's results.

As they approached the executive wing, the prince paused. "You haven't mentioned how you feel about Giselle's news."

Had she said something about their breakup after all? "I'm not sure what news you mean," Bryce said warily.

The prince's smile sharpened. "I might have known she wouldn't give me the credit, although the loophole wouldn't have been found without my equerry's persistence. He has an interest in old documents, and spotted a detail the lawyers managed to miss."

Bryce was still bemused. "Loophole?"

"In the Merrisand Charter. I thought Giselle would have been eager to share the news with you, since she's the beneficiary."

Evidently not eager enough. "We've both been busy," Bryce dissembled.

Max grinned. "I've never had a Wedding Eve, but I can understand how busy might define it."

"You'd better fill me in," Bryce said, wondering why he felt so sure he wasn't going to like it.

He soon found out.

"The lawyers looked in the wrong place," Max stated. "The charter itself clearly states that only a married woman may become Keeper of the Castle. But my equerry discovered a codicil that allows for a single woman to succeed to the job provided she has done the work for, quote, 'a thousand days without recompense.' Giselle's voluntary teaching work at the castle school and the long, unpaid hours she has put in on the trust's behalf for the last eight years means she undoubtedly qualifies."

A chill snaked down Bryce's spine. "And she knew about the codicil before our Wedding Eve?"

"Perhaps she wants the news to come as a surprise."

"It's certainly that." In more ways than the prince could possibly imagine.

Max inclined his head. "I hope I haven't spoiled it for her."

"I doubt it. I was on my way to see her. You've given us a great deal to talk about."

Max gave a regal shrug. "Women. You'd think she would be eager to share such news with you. I'm sure she has her own reasons for keeping it to herself."

A guard snapped off a crisp salute as Max bounded up the stone steps. Left alone, Bryce stood for a moment, collecting his scattered wits. He didn't doubt that Giselle had good reasons for not telling him her news. None of those reasons were destined to make him feel good.

She had known that she qualified for the job of Keeper before they set off on their Wedding Eve. She must have become alarmed when Bryce allowed his passion full rein, and decided to end it there and then, since she didn't need him anymore.

And Bryce had stupidly convinced himself she had fallen in love with him.

He had been right all along. Love was a risky business he was better off without. Just as well he'd learned the truth before he bared his soul to her.

In this grim mood, he stormed into the conservatory. The class was just ending. He kept his temper in check long enough to arrange for Amanda to go home with Mary Jo, waited until the room cleared, then slammed the door shut.

"Is there any glass left in that?" she asked mildly, her only response to the reverberating slam.

"If I did what I'm inclined to do, there wouldn't be," he snapped. Slamming the door had seemed preferable to putting his fist through it.

She did look up then, and her lovely eyes clouded with apprehension when she saw his face. If he looked half as angry as he felt, no wonder she looked scared, but he resisted the temptation to soften his mood. If he did, he might take her in his arms and make an even bigger fool of himself than he'd already done.

She went around the conservatory, collecting up art materials, although he was sure she had servants to do that. Perhaps she just needed to be busy. "Is something wrong?" she asked.

He loomed over the top of an easel, forcing her to look at him. "You could say that. I ran into Max outside, and he told me about the codicil."

He saw her swallow hard. "Oh."

Rounding the easel, he lifted a fistful of brushes

out of her hand and set them down, turning her so she couldn't avoid his accusing gaze. "Now I understand why you called the wedding off. You had no need to see it through because you'd already gotten what you wanted, hadn't you?"

For a moment, fire blazed in her eyes. She tugged her hands free and planted them on her hips. "If you believe that, then you're the biggest idiot in the kingdom."

He hadn't expected her to attack him, Giselle saw as she seethed with white-hot fury of her own. How dare he accuse her of using him, then abandoning him when he no longer served her purpose? How immoral did he think she was?

Her breathing shallowed, reducing her intended shout to a husky statement. "If you must know, I spent the morning drafting a letter to Max and the board declining to become Keeper of the Castle."

If she had stabbed him with one of the paintbrushes, his shock couldn't have been more manifest. "You're turning the position down?"

"Not the position, only the title. I decided I don't need it to go on doing work I love with all my heart."

"Does your decision have anything to do with me?" he asked, sounding shaken.

Pleased that she had rattled his cage, she barely stopped a smile. "How you flatter yourself. First you accuse me of wanting to marry you purely to satisfy my ambition. Now you also want to claim responsibility because my priorities have changed. Has it occurred to you that I might make a few decisions on my own account?"

"Such as refusing to marry me?"

She clasped her hands together so he wouldn't see

how badly they were trembling. "That was one of them."

"Care to tell me why?"

She dropped her lashes to hide her gaze, but not quickly enough. On a sharply indrawn breath, he closed the distance between them and took her in his arms. "I don't want to be accused of hubris again, but is there any chance at all that you've fallen in love with me?"

She held herself rigid, resisting the temptation to soften against him, afraid that if she did, she wouldn't be able to stop until she had found his mouth and drunk her fill. "You made it plain enough that you don't want love," she whispered.

He lifted her hand and brushed the back with his lips, the contact searing through her as acutely as if he'd touched her with flame. "As you've just proved with the Keeper's job, we don't always know ourselves what we truly want," he observed.

"I knew," she said around a huge lump clogging her throat. "That was my dilemma."

He nodded, looking troubled. "A dilemma of my causing." When she made a sound of protest, he shook his head. "Not pride this time, only acceptance of fact. You wanted to be a wife in more than name, am I right?"

She didn't want him to be right, but she couldn't look away. "Yes, damn you."

"And since I didn't appear to want the same thing, you called a halt."

Frustration built inside her and she whirled away from him, putting a table set with a still life between them. "Will your infernal pride be satisfied if I confess that I made the colossal mistake of falling in love with you?''

He glared at her. ''My pride would be better satisfied if your confession was in the present tense.''

Being speechless was rare in her experience, but it threatened her now. She fought it, refusing to let him reduce her to the tears that hovered close to the surface. They weren't tears of sadness, she knew, as hope welled. ''All right, I love you in the present tense,'' she snapped.

He moved around the table, making the delicately balanced fruit arrangement tremble. She stood her ground. This time his hold was gentle, persuasive and not to be resisted. ''Say that again,'' he insisted.

''Why should I?'' she demanded.

''Because I don't want to be the only one feeling this way.''

She could hardly breathe. ''You're not. Walking away from you was the hardest thing I've ever done.''

''Not turning down the job of Keeper?''

She tensed, before conceding that it was a fair question. ''I'd made up my mind to do that before I came to you on our Wedding Eve. I wanted to tell you, but I was afraid of betraying how I really felt about you.''

''And I behaved like a moron, insisting that I didn't want your love. Can you forgive me, and believe that I love you?''

''As long as I know that, I can forgive you anything,'' she said, heartfelt.

His eyes misted. ''I've loved you since my first sight of you at the masked ball, injured but determined not to give in to weakness.'' He touched a finger to her lashes, where she felt tears hovering there. "Then you confronted me on Amanda's behalf, like a tigress defending a cub who wasn't even hers."

She stirred in his arms. "Did you say anything to her about us?"

"As far as she knows, nothing has changed. You and I are going to be married and live happily ever after."

"And are we?"

"That depends."

Fear shivered through her. "On what?"

"On whether you still want me. I'm a stubborn, prideful man and I haven't the least idea how to behave as the husband of a princess. You'll have a lot to teach me." He drew a shuddering breath. "You've already taught me a great deal, starting with how to love again."

She touched the back of her hand to his cheek, the slight abrasiveness of his skin contrasting deliciously with her own softness. "You needed no lessons, only a helping hand to find what you'd mislaid for a time. As to the other—" she waved the hand dismissively "—the royal family is a work-in-progress. You'll bring your own style to the role of prince, and our family will be the stronger for it."

"I'm glad you think so," he said, his features relaxing into a smile. "There is, however, one other thing I require before we resume our engagement."

She studied his face, feeling uncertainty grip her. "What would that be?"

"You're to accept the job of Keeper of the Castle. You've worked for it, you deserve it, and I want you to have it."

Joy spun through her like quicksilver. She'd meant what she'd said about being glad to do the work without the recognition. She still felt she needed no official title to devote her heart to the trust. But for Bryce's sake, she would accept. "Yes, my liege," she intoned.

He laughed delightedly. "I like the sound of that."

"Don't get too used to it," she cautioned. "The Keeper outranks the controller of the Royal Deer Park."

"Of *my* deer park," he amended. "Frankly, I don't care if I have to bow before you in public. I'm man enough to do that as protocol requires. As long as we have an equal relationship behind closed doors."

Thinking of the relationship they would enjoy behind closed doors, she quivered with anticipation. Royal weddings weren't arranged overnight. How was she to contain herself until they could lie in one another's arms as man and wife? "What we do in private will be our concern and no one else's," she assured him.

His hold tightened and his mouth lowered to hers. "I like the sound of that, too."

Losing herself in the exquisite pleasure of his kiss, she let her response speak for her, knowing there was no more powerful declaration of love in all the world.

Epilogue

A glow of happiness washed over Giselle as she watched the crowd of elegantly dressed guests move around the gallery. Her father, Prince Gabriel, had officially opened the Voyager Exhibition a short time before. She could see his dark, leonine head close to her mother's as they studied one of the major works, the first European map accurately showing the islands of Carramer in relation to its South Pacific neighbors.

With them was Giselle's cousin, Rowe Sevrin, and his new bride, the former Kirsten Bond. In her previous role, Kirsten had curated the exhibition. Now she was visiting it as Viscountess Aragon. Their adorable six-year-old son, Jeffrey, held tight to his parents' hands, more fascinated by trays of canapés carried around by the servants than by the priceless exhibits around him.

Kirsten looked as starry-eyed as Giselle felt, the princess mused as her gaze unerringly found Bryce. He was showing Amanda around the exhibition, and love for him and his beautiful child almost stopped her heart.

They were going to be a family. Her family. Could any feeling in the world be more special than the way she felt right now?

She jumped as her brother spoke close to her ear. "Rowe and Kirsten must be feeling pretty pleased with themselves. Their brilliant organization of the Tour de Merrisand has not only ensured the trust will have sufficient funds for its work for years to come, they've also raised the public profile of the castle, so that exhibitions like Voyager will be real crowd pullers."

Giselle nodded. Kirsten had confided how hard she had resisted Rowe's plan to stage a major cycling race around the castle and environs. Falling in love with her viscount had helped to change her mind, she had admitted. Giselle knew exactly how she felt.

"Something tells me that look of pure joy I can see in your eyes isn't because the exhibition looks like a blockbuster," Max observed.

Her radiant smile forgave her brother his ignorance. "When you fall in love, you'll understand how amazing it feels."

The prince's smile faded and he took a sip of champagne. "Not much chance of that, is there?"

Immediately filled with remorse, she touched his arm. "Oh, Max, this must be hard for you." Preoccupied with her love for Bryce, she had overlooked the Champagne Pact, an ancient agreement that meant the heir to Taures could only marry a woman of royal blood. Her voice softened. "You never know, you might find a princess to fall madly in love with."

His gaze swept the gallery. "And there are so many for me to choose from."

She moved closer, lowering her voice for his ears alone. "I never thought I'd find love so close to home, but I did. So can you."

"Even if Father has to bestow a title on her, to fulfill the conditions of the pact," Max commented dryly.

She laughed, diffusing some of her unease. "Now there's an idea."

"Somehow, I doubt it's that simple, or the pact would have ceased to have any force years ago."

In the end, it had been simple for her, Giselle thought. But then she wasn't bound by a contract made by her forebears, decreeing that everything she held dear would be sacrificed if she should fall in love with the wrong person. As the first-born son of Taures, that was Max's burden. Still, he had found a loophole for her. Why wouldn't one exist for him? It might be more difficult to find, but her brother would find it if anyone could.

Bryce saw her and started toward her. Her pulse set up an erratic tattoo. In the end things would work out for Max, too. They had to. "It's not fair," she murmured. "You've worked harder for the Merrisand Trust than anyone else. You deserve your chance at happiness."

"I'm happy enough as I am," he assured her, although the sudden tightening around his eyes contradicted the assertion. "Next you'll be reminding me of the legend that says anyone who serves the trust is rewarded by finding true love."

"It worked for me." The love she saw every time

she looked into Bryce's eyes was all the proof she needed.

The prince thrust a hand into the pocket of his jacket. "You took your time realizing it."

"I was a fool," she hissed, earning a look of curiosity from her brother. "I thought all I had to do was my work for the trust, and the legend would grant me my heart's desire."

The prince's glance went from Bryce back to her. "It did, didn't it?"

"Not until I committed my heart to the trust, and that didn't happen until I was willing to give up my ambition to become Keeper of the Castle and simply serve to the best of my ability." Amazingly, as soon as she did, she not only gained Bryce's love but a way opened for her to achieve her goal. Mysterious ways, indeed.

Max surrendered his champagne glass to a passing footman, then turned to her. "I'm happy for you and Bryce, Giselle. I'm also happy doing what I do. I don't need anything else to make my life complete."

But he did need some*one* else, she thought. Everyone did. Too bad he was right, eligible princesses were a rare commodity these days. That didn't mean love was impossible for her brother. Only more of a challenge than for most other people. He had never shirked a challenge in his life, and she didn't doubt he would find a way if—when—the right woman came along. Love would show him the way, as it had done for her and Bryce.

Wasn't that the promise of the Merrisand legend?

Her view of the man she loved was veiled as her eyes suddenly misted. She blinked furiously to clear her vision, recognizing the tears as gratitude for a future so bright it took her breath away.

"You look radiant tonight, my love," Bryce said, taking her hand.

Warmth flooded through her as she threaded her fingers through his. With her other hand, she reached out for Amanda. Out of the corner of her eye, she saw her mother, Princess Marie, give a tiny frown at her daughter's public display of affection.

Too happy to be provoked, Giselle smiled back brilliantly and was astonished to see her mother's expression soften. To Giselle's amazement, Marie shot Giselle a mischievous look, then slipped her arm into her husband's before they walked on.

There was no doubt about it, Giselle thought. The power of love was infinite. Max was so sure that it wasn't for him. Until she met Bryce, she would have said the same. Now she didn't dare try to predict what might happen. She only knew it would be more thrilling than anything they could possibly imagine.

* * * * *

Prince Maxim may have resigned himself to never marrying for love, but the Merrisand Trust has been proven to inspire miracles! Will Maxim meet his match? Find out next month in THE PRINCE AND THE MARRIAGE PACT, RS #1699.

SILHOUETTE **Romance**®

Valerie Parv, official historian to
the Carramer crown,
returns to the island kingdom
in her new miniseries

THE CARRAMER TRUST

It was said that those who served the Carramer Trust
would find true love...but could the legend
marry off these royals?

THE VISCOUNT & THE VIRGIN

Silhouette Romance #1691,
available October 2003

THE PRINCESS & THE MASKED MAN

Silhouette Romance #1695,
available November 2003

THE PRINCE & THE MARRIAGE PACT

Silhouette Romance #1699,
available December 2003

Available at your favorite retail outlet.

✂

Your opinion is important to us! Please take a few moments to share your thoughts with us about your experiences with Harlequin and Silhouette books. Your comments will be very useful in ensuring that we deliver books you love to read.
Please take a few minutes to complete the questionnaire, then send it to us at the address below.

Send your completed questionnaires to:
Harlequin/Silhouette Reader Survey, P.O. Box 9046, Buffalo, NY 14269-9046

1. As you may know, there are many different lines under the Harlequin and Silhouette brands. Each of the lines is listed below. Please check the box that most represents your reading habit for each line.

Line	Currently read this line	Do not read this line	Not sure if I read this line
Harlequin American Romance	❏	❏	❏
Harlequin Duets	❏	❏	❏
Harlequin Romance	❏	❏	❏
Harlequin Historicals	❏	❏	❏
Harlequin Superromance	❏	❏	❏
Harlequin Intrigue	❏	❏	❏
Harlequin Presents	❏	❏	❏
Harlequin Temptation	❏	❏	❏
Harlequin Blaze	❏	❏	❏
Silhouette Special Edition	❏	❏	❏
Silhouette Romance	❏	❏	❏
Silhouette Intimate Moments	❏	❏	❏
Silhouette Desire	❏	❏	❏

2. Which of the following best describes why you bought *this book?* One answer only, please.

the picture on the cover	❏	the title	❏
the author	❏	the line is one I read often	❏
part of a miniseries	❏	saw an ad in another book	❏
saw an ad in a magazine/newsletter	❏	a friend told me about it	❏
I borrowed/was given this book	❏	other: _____	❏

3. Where did you buy *this book?* One answer only, please.

at Barnes & Noble	❏	at a grocery store	❏
at Waldenbooks	❏	at a drugstore	❏
at Borders	❏	on eHarlequin.com Web site	❏
at another bookstore	❏	from another Web site	❏
at Wal-Mart	❏	Harlequin/Silhouette Reader	❏
at Target	❏	Service/through the mail	
at Kmart	❏	used books from anywhere	❏
at another department store or mass merchandiser	❏	I borrowed/was given this book	❏

4. On average, how many Harlequin and Silhouette books do you buy at one time?

I buy _____ books at one time	❏
I rarely buy a book	❏

MRQ403SR-1A

5. How many times per month do you shop for any *Harlequin and/or Silhouette* books?
One answer only, please.

1 or more times a week	❏	a few times per year	❏
1 to 3 times per month	❏	less often than once a year	❏
1 to 2 times every 3 months	❏	never	❏

6. When you think of your ideal heroine, which *one* statement describes her the best?
One answer only, please.

She's a woman who is strong-willed	❏	She's a desirable woman	❏
She's a woman who is needed by others	❏	She's a powerful woman	❏
She's a woman who is taken care of	❏	She's a passionate woman	❏
She's an adventurous woman	❏	She's a sensitive woman	❏

7. The following statements describe types or genres of books that you may be
interested in reading. Pick *up to 2 types* of books that you are most interested in.

I like to read about truly romantic relationships	❏
I like to read stories that are sexy romances	❏
I like to read romantic comedies	❏
I like to read a romantic mystery/suspense	❏
I like to read about romantic adventures	❏
I like to read romance stories that involve family	❏
I like to read about a romance in times or places that I have never seen	❏
Other: _____	❏

*The following questions help us to group your answers with those readers who are
similar to you. Your answers will remain confidential.*

8. Please record your year of birth below.

19 _____

9. What is your marital status?

single ❏   married ❏   common-law ❏   widowed ❏
divorced/separated ❏

10. Do you have children 18 years of age or younger currently living at home?

yes ❏   no ❏

11. Which of the following best describes your employment status?

employed full-time or part-time ❏   homemaker ❏   student ❏
retired ❏   unemployed ❏

12. Do you have access to the Internet from either home or work?

yes ❏   no ❏

13. Have you ever visited eHarlequin.com?

yes ❏   no ❏

14. What state do you live in?

_____

15. Are you a member of Harlequin/Silhouette Reader Service?

yes ❏   Account # _____   no ❏   MRQ403SR-1B

If you enjoyed what you just read,
then we've got an offer you can't resist!

Take 2 bestselling
love stories FREE!
Plus get a FREE surprise gift!

Clip this page and mail it to Silhouette Reader Service

IN U.S.A.	IN CANADA
3010 Walden Ave.	P.O. Box 609
P.O. Box 1867	Fort Erie, Ontario
Buffalo, N.Y. 14240-1867	L2A 5X3

YES! Please send me 2 free Silhouette Romance® novels and my free surprise gift. After receiving them, if I don't wish to receive anymore, I can return the shipping statement marked cancel. If I don't cancel, I will receive 6 brand-new novels every month, before they're available in stores! In the U.S.A., bill me at the bargain price of $21.34 per shipment plus 25¢ shipping and handling per book and applicable sales tax, if any*. In Canada, bill me at the bargain price of $24.68 plus 25¢ shipping and handling per book and applicable taxes**. That's the complete price and a savings of at least 10% off the cover prices—what a great deal! I understand that accepting the 2 free books and gift places me under no obligation ever to buy any books. I can always return a shipment and cancel at any time. Even if I never buy another book from Silhouette, the 2 free books and gift are mine to keep forever.

209 SDN DU9H
309 SDN DU9J

Name	(PLEASE PRINT)	
Address	Apt.#	
City	State/Prov.	Zip/Postal Code

* Terms and prices subject to change without notice. Sales tax applicable in N.Y.
** Canadian residents will be charged applicable provincial taxes and GST.
  All orders subject to approval. Offer limited to one per household and not valid to current Silhouette Romance® subscribers.
  ® are registered trademarks of Harlequin Books S.A., used under license.

SROM03   ©1998 Harlequin Enterprises Limited

eHARLEQUIN.com

The eHarlequin.com online community is *the* place to share opinions, thoughts and feelings!

- Joining the community is easy, fun and **FREE!**

- Connect with **other romance fans** on our message boards.

- Meet your **favorite authors** without leaving home!

- **Share opinions** on books, movies, celebrities…and *more!*

Here's what our members say:

"I love the friendly and helpful atmosphere filled with support and humor."
—Texanna (eHarlequin.com member)

"Is this the place for me, or what? There is nothing I love more than 'talking' books, especially with fellow readers who are reading the same ones I am."
—Jo Ann (eHarlequin.com member)

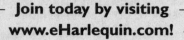

Join today by visiting
www.eHarlequin.com!

INTCOMM

SILHOUETTE *Romance*®

COMING NEXT MONTH

#1698 SANTA BROUGHT A SON—Melissa McClone
Marrying the Boss's Daughter

An old friend's wedding had brought Reed Connors back home—and face-to-face with Samantha Wilson. Determined not to let the one-who-got-away get away a second time, he vowed to win her heart. But then he met Samantha's young son whose striking resemblance to Reed was undeniable. Had Santa brought the lonely VP the most precious gift of all: a family?

#1699 THE PRINCE & THE MARRIAGE PACT—Valerie Parv
The Carramer Trust

Annegret West was unimpressed with titled men and majestic trappings, but somehow His Royal Heartthrob Prince Maxim de Marigny made her jaded heart flutter! Yet despite her growing emotional attachment, she knew Maxim must marry a princess or forfeit his throne. If only she had been born royal....

#1700 THE BACHELOR'S DARE—Shirley Jump

Ladies' man Mark Dole and down-on-her-luck Claire Richards both had the same goal: win the "Survive and Drive" contest's grand prize, an RV, to fund their future dreams. But could these childhood enemies put aside their competitive natures and work together to win? And would a crazy contest end with good old-fashioned romance in an RV for the playboy and the hairdresser?

#1701 THE NANNY'S PLAN—Donna Clayton

Workaholic professor Pierce Kincaid may have agreed to baby-sit his six-year-old nephews for the summer, but he certainly wasn't going to do it alone! Enter Amy Edwards, the temporary take-charge nanny he hired to tame the rambunctious twins. It looked like Pierce's not-so-quiet summer was going to be an adventure in life—and love!